Fic
App

Yar

The
Devil's
Highway

The Devil's Highway

Stan Applegate

Illustrated by
James Watling

PEACHTREE
ATLANTA

A Peachtree Junior Publication

Published by
PEACHTREE PUBLISHERS, LTD.
1700 Chattahoochee Avenue
Atlanta, Georgia 30318-2112

www.peachtree-online.com

Book design by Dana L. Laurent and Loraine M. Balcsik
Composition by Melanie M. McMahon

Manufactured in the United States of America

10 9 8 7 6 5 4 3

Library of Congress Cataloging-in-Publication Data

Applegate, Stanley.
The devil's highway / by Stanley Applegate ; illustrated by James Watling.—1st ed.
p. cm.
Summary: In 1811, on the Natchez Road, fourteen-year-old Zeb finds ten-year-old Hannah, who has been
kidnapped from her Choctaw people, and together they face natural and human threats with their combined skills
and courage.
ISBN 1-56145-184-3
[1.Natchez Trace--Fiction. 2. Frontier and pioneer life—Fiction. 3. Choctaw Indians—Fiction. 4. Indians of
North America—Fiction.] I. Watling, James, ill. II. Title.
PZ7.A6487Dg 1998
[Fic]—dc21
                                                                98-22720
                                                                    CIP
                                                                    AC

For my wife, Marjorie

ACKNOWLEDGMENTS

I wish to thank Carol Lee Lorenzo and the Children's Writing Group at Emory University for all of their help and encouragement.

I also wish to thank Sarah Helyar Smith, my editor at Peachtree Publishers, for her guidance and support, and my agent Joan Brandt for her warm enthusiasm and her advocacy.

For their assistance on historical research, I am indebted to James Crutchfield and the Williamson County Public Library; the National Park Service staff at the Natchez Trace Parkway; the Historic Natchez Foundation; the Natchez Public Library; Meyers Brown of the Atlanta History Center; the Mississippi Department of Archives and History; Bob Ferguson and the Choctaw Museum in Philadelphia, Mississippi; and Ken Knopp for his help on horses and saddles of the period.

Table of
CONTENTS

CHAPTER ONE

Pursuit

Franklin, Tennessee
September 5, 1811

Zeb pulled the sweaty horse to a stop at the edge of the forest. He turned in the saddle and stared down the steep meadow into the valley below, searching for any movement. In the distance he could just make out the house and barns of his family's farm, silent and abandoned in the moonlight.

About a half mile down the valley, lanterns still glowed in the windows of Tate McPhee's ramshackle cabin. "Must still be celebrating," he whispered to the horse. "They don't know we've gone."

The horse stomped his foot in the tall grass. Zeb leaned forward until his mouth was next to the horse's ear. "Hush, Christmas," he said. "We gotta be real quiet." He turned the big horse, moving into the dark forest at a slow, careful walk. Even with a full moon rising, he couldn't see more than a few feet ahead of him.

The horse skidded down the embankment onto the Natchez Road. The road was overgrown, just wide enough for one horse and rider or for men walking single file. Zeb grimaced. The muffled plop plop of the horse's hooves on the leaf-covered dirt road seemed loud after the almost silent canter up through the meadow.

He hated to dismount now, but there was no other way. He stroked the horse's neck, talking quietly with him. "No point riding any farther, Christmas," he whispered. "Can't see a thing. Don't want you to step in a hole." He slipped off the horse and led him down the Natchez Road.

As they walked, the horse turned his head, looking down at him. Zeb prayed Christmas would keep quiet. It was not only Tate McPhee's men who worried him. Bands of outlaws hid in the forest waiting for people traveling alone. If they found him, they would take his horse and saddle and all of his belongings. He'd be lucky if they left him alive.

Zeb led Christmas for about an hour, trying to put distance between him and McPhee's men. He wondered what they would do to him if they found him.

He peered into the dark forest. The light from the rising moon was beginning to penetrate the dense canopy overhead. The road was easier to see, but it was still too risky to ride. He spotted a huge fallen oak not far from the trail. The long, moss-covered trunk was almost as wide as he was tall. A clump of river birches grew nearby. "We'll be able to hide over there and get some rest," Zeb whispered, stroking the horse. "We've got to be real quiet."

Zeb led him up onto the forest floor and around the fallen trunk. The moon was much brighter now. He could see a little clearing bordered on one side by the fallen tree and on the other by the clump of birches.

He stood the rifle and one of the old dueling pistols against the trunk of the big tree, leaving the other pistol in his belt, just in case. He untied the bedroll from the back of the saddle. The canvas cover was wrapped around his cooking pots. He stretched the canvas on the ground and then unpacked the battered tinware pots, careful to make as little noise as possible.

A long, narrow loaf of bread fell out of the bedroll. He broke off a piece and bit through the hard crust, smiling at the familiar taste. His mama had made the bread the day before, filling the cabin with the smell of yeast as she kneaded the dough and then formed the bread into the long loaves his daddy had always liked.

He was tempted to eat more, but he had a long way to go, maybe a month of riding if he were lucky. Better just to eat a little now and save the rest.

He left the bedroll, the saddle, and his two saddlebags on the canvas sheet and walked the horse through the blanket of last year's dead leaves to the grove of birches. His grampa had always told him that these little birch clumps were the only places in the deep forest where there was enough grass for grazing. He squinched his eyes closed. *Please let Grampa be alive,* he prayed.

The horse lowered his head over Zeb's shoulder. He reached up and stroked the soft muzzle. "I'll give you some grain tomorrow morning, Christmas. Gotta leave at first light."

As he tied Christmas to a low branch, he heard a metallic clang. It sounded like his pots and pans banging together! Had McPhee's men caught up with him already? He pulled the old dueling pistol out of his belt, ready to climb back on Christmas and ride away from there. He stood still, listening.... Not a sound.... He crept back to where he had left his gear.

A girl who looked to be about ten years old was crouching near his bedroll, motionless, wary, ready to run at the slightest movement.

3

When she saw the pistol in his hand, she dropped the bread.

She had been eating his loaf of bread. She clutched the bread against her chest as if she were afraid he would take it from her. When he moved, she turned to run, but the fallen tree was in her way.

He ran toward her, waving his pistol. "Hey! You there!" he said in a loud whisper. "What do you think you're doing?"

The girl cringed. She held one arm in front of her as if she thought he would hit her. When she saw the pistol in his hand, she dropped the bread and spat out what she was eating. "Please don't shoot me, mister," she whispered. "I won't eat any more."

Zeb stood taller, looking down at the girl. No one had ever called him "mister" before.

The girl put her finger to her lips. She pleaded with her eyes for him to be quiet. He nodded and turned his head slowly, looking for any movement in the shadows. He turned back to the girl.

She looked like some wild creature of the forest. Her short black hair stuck out from her head in every direction. She was wearing a homespun dress, torn in places and caked with dried mud, the coarse, loose weave stretched longer on one side. It was hard to see in the dark, but it seemed to him that her spindly arms and legs were gray with dirt.

He lowered the pistol. "I ain't gonna shoot you," he whispered. "Go ahead and eat. Looks like you're starving. What're you doing here anyway?"

Zeb suddenly remembered what his uncle Ira had said about children being used as bait on the Natchez Road. He put his back to the tree, waving his pistol slowly back and forth. His mouth was dry. He could hardly speak. "Where's your gang?" he whispered.

She shifted a wad of bread to one side of her mouth. "I don't know," she said, swallowing. Her eyes darted around the forest. "I hope I never see them again."

"So you do belong to a gang." He stooped to pick up the other pistol.

"I did, but I don't now," she said, sitting down on the blanket. "I ran away." She stuffed another piece of the bread in her mouth.

"You ran away? How do I know you're telling the truth? Why were you with a gang?"

"They stole me down at Yowani to work the Natchez Road."

He didn't believe anything she was saying. He kept looking around, expecting outlaws to appear from behind every tree. He was sure that he had caught her in a lie. "You were living at Yowani? That's Choctaw country. That's only for Indians."

"Not only for Indians," she said. "There are Indians and whites there. Most of us are Indian, though."

"You don't look like an Indian. What's your name, anyway?"

"My name is Hannah McAllister."

"But that's not Indian!"

"Well, I'm half Indian," she said. "My mama's Choctaw. My father's a white man, a doctor. He works with the Choctaw medicine men at Yowani, learnin' from them and sharin' what he knows."

She looked down at the clothes she was wearing. "When I'm in Yowani, I feel Choctaw. I dress like a Choctaw. The outlaws made me wear this dress. They stole it from some farmer's clothesline. Said it made me look more like a white child." She pulled the hem of the dress down toward her ankles. "Too small for me now."

She ran her fingers through the wild mess on her head. "The outlaws didn't like Indians," she said. "That's why they cut off my hair. I had kept it in a beautiful long braid down my back."

Zeb couldn't help but smile. This tough little person had tears in her eyes because they had cut her hair.

"They said nobody was gonna stop if I was nothin' but an Indian," she said. "I was s'posed to look like a white child, lost in the woods. Is it true? Do you think nobody would stop for a lost Indian child?"

"I think nobody stops at all anymore," he said. "Everybody's heard about luring travelers on the Natchez Road with women or little children."

She seemed to be weighing what he said. She nodded as if she didn't notice that he had evaded her question.

"Why did they kidnap you? What happened?" he insisted.

She sighed. "Mama warned me not to go near the woods."

"And?..."

She yawned and rubbed her eyes. "And I did. I thought I heard a baby crying. But it was a man. An outlaw. He grabbed me and covered my mouth. He carried me into the woods. I bit his hand as hard as I could. He just held me tighter until I couldn't breathe."

Zeb shook his head. There was a good possibility that she was telling the truth, but that just made things more complicated. What was he going to do with her? It might be nice to have someone to travel with, but if Tate McPhee's men got him, they'd get her too. They couldn't afford to leave anybody alive. He looked down at her upturned face. She seemed to be trying to read his thoughts. "And then what happened?" he asked more gently.

"He took me to a place in the forest. There was a gang of outlaws. Not only men. Four of the men had women with them, and there were three little children, just babies. They said I had to help them work the Natchez Road."

"They wanted you to stand on the Natchez Road and cry and try to stop travelers." He shook his head. "Isn't anyone looking for you?"

"I'm sure that Father and some of the *tushka,* the Choctaw warriors, came lookin' for me right away, but the gang moved up here into Chickasaw territory. The Choctaw won't come up here."

"You think your daddy gave up?"

Hannah turned her face away from him. "It's been almost six months," she said. "They stole me last March. When you get kidnapped by the outlaws, you're never seen again. That's just the way it is. Everybody knows that."

"But somehow you got away."

"Been plannin' it for a long time," she whispered, about to push another piece of bread into her mouth. "I heard them makin' plans to go up to a place just north of Franklin to wait for somebody important coming down from Nashville with a lot of money. They said they'd have to stay up there for a while, so I figured that would give me a chance to get away. They'll go north and I'll go south. If I can walk about twenty miles a day, I can get to Yowani in maybe two or three weeks."

Zeb sat down next to her on the canvas. "Doubt you could make twenty miles a day," he said. "Hafta spend half of your time just looking for food. How long you been running from them?"

"Just started," she said, looking over her shoulder into the deep woods around them. "If you'd a' come along a few hours sooner you'd a' met the gang right here," she said. "They were

8

packin' up, gettin' ready to leave, and I just slipped away. I could hear them huntin' for me all over the place. Said they'd skin me alive if they caught me."

Zeb peered again into the dark forest, searching for movements in the shadows. He looked down at the bread in the girl's hand. "You were eating that bread like you hadn't eaten in a week."

Hannah nodded. "We were runnin' out of food. The men eat first and give what's left to the women and children. There hasn't been much. I hope you don't hold it against me, mister. I was hungry."

"Now what are you going to do?"

"Can I come with you? I can ride just about anything. That plow horse of yours looks big enough to hold us both."

Zeb looked at her, not at all sure what to do.

Hannah moved to grab his arm, then pulled back, as if she were not sure she should touch him. She dropped her hand to her lap. "Please, mister," she said, "I don't want that gang of outlaws to find me. If they catch me, they'll near kill me." She turned her head away from him.

Zeb could see that she was trying to keep from crying. *Can't leave her*, he thought, *but taking her with me is really going to slow me down. She probably can't ride at all.*

"Listen," he said in a low voice, "I'll take you as far as the first stand. You can stay there. They'll take care of you."

She looked back at him with a sharp intake of breath, almost a sob.

"I can't take you all the way down to Yowani," he said, scowling at her. "I just can't lose any more time. With two people it'll take a lot longer. I've got to get to Natchez in a hurry, and I'm only a few hours ahead of real trouble."

She shrank away from him. "You an outlaw?" she whispered. Zeb shook his head. "No. I'm not. I'll tell you all about it later." She handed him the last piece of bread. "We better get going."

He stuck the bread in his pocket. "We can't go tonight," he whispered. "Too dark for Christmas. Grampa says they haven't cleared that trail in almost ten years. We'll sleep here and leave at first light in the morning."

She smiled. "You call that big nag *Christmas?*"

Zeb nodded. "Got him for Christmas almost four years ago. Fastest horse in Franklin, Tennessee. Nobody's ever beat him."

Hannah cut her eyes up at Zeb as if he were a teller of tall tales. A gust of wind rustled the leaves above them. She looked around the forest, the smile disappearing from her face. "I don't even know your name," she said.

"My name is Zebulon D'Evereux," he said. "Everybody calls me Zeb."

TWO

The Devil's Backbone

Hannah stood up and brushed the bread crumbs from her dress. "I'll be right back," she said. She disappeared into the dark without making a sound. Zeb shrugged and lay back on the canvas. *That's going to be one more complication,* he thought. *She'll probably need to stop every half hour to pee. What have I gotten myself into?*

The girl came back as silently as she had gone. She leaned down and whispered to him, "There's a little brook down there, if you want to water your horse."

Zeb led Christmas down to the creek. When he returned he could barely see Hannah in the dark. She was sitting down, leaning against a tree, the back of her legs resting on a soft carpet of moss. Her eyes were closed and she appeared to be asleep. When Zeb stepped into the clearing, her eyes flew open. "Sorry," she whispered, leaping to her feet, "I haven't really slept all that much for a while. I should have been keeping lookout."

Zeb looked down at her, wondering how he could ever have doubted her. "You take that blanket and find a comfortable place to sleep. I'll take the horse blanket and the canvas."

She walked slowly around the campsite, holding the folded blanket against her chest. A carpet of brown leaves covered the forest floor. Clumps of ferns grew in the low places. She circled around the moss-covered area a couple of times and then shook her head. Except for the clump of birches, this part of the forest had very little undergrowth. The fallen oak provided the only protection.

She spread the blanket next to the fallen oak, rolled it around herself, and closed her eyes. Zeb took off his hat and hung it on the branch of a shrub nearby. He stretched out on the canvas and stared up into the branches of the tall trees silhouetted against the moonlit sky. This was the first time he had had a moment to stop and think.

Only a few hours ago, he and McPhee had stood nose to nose, shouting at each other. He had called McPhee a liar. He said that he would go and look for Grampa himself. McPhee's face was purple with rage. Zeb could still hear his words: "Go ahead and try it! A boy like you wouldn't make it one night on the Natchez Road."

That impulse to scare McPhee had been stupid. Now McPhee would know exactly where he had gone. If his men weren't too drunk, they could even be on their way tonight.

Hannah was going to be a big responsibility. He turned to look at her. Her eyes were wide open now, watching him. *Must be wondering if she can trust me*, he thought. *Probably still thinks I'm an outlaw.*

It was so quiet he could hear the scratching of wood mice under the blanket of leaves. Did Hannah know that there were panthers and bears in this area? He wished he could build a fire, but a fire would tell McPhee's men just where they were. Stretching out his hand to be sure that the rifle and the two pistols were within easy reach, he closed his eyes and tried to sleep.

He awoke early the next morning to the loud tapping of a woodpecker nearby. Tiny beads of dew shimmered like jewels on spiderwebs stretched across the ferns. The familiar loamy smell of dead oak leaves and the bitter smell of ferns reminded him of hunting trips with his grampa. He sat up and looked around.

The trunk of the oak tree hid them from anyone following on the Natchez Road. He looked toward the birches. No one on the Natchez Road would be able to see Christmas.

His mouth dropped open as his eyes passed over the mossy spot where Hannah had been sitting. Three fairy rings of wild mushrooms glistened with dew. He recalled his mother saying that where fairies danced in the forest at night, rings of mushrooms grew the next morning.

Zeb felt the hair on the back of his neck stand on end. Hannah stood with the rolled blanket in her arms, watching him. He looked over at the fairy rings and then back at her.

The girl had followed his glance. She grinned and whispered, "Maybe I am and maybe I ain't."

Even in the early morning light, it was still too dark in the forest to know what time it was. "We better leave as soon as possible," he said quietly. "If you need to go, now's the time."

Hannah went down to the brook. When she got back, her face was clean, and her arms and legs were still wet from where she had tried to scrub up. She turned away from him.

Zeb winced at the swollen, red switch marks on the backs of her legs.

They repacked the pots and pans with the little pieces of cloth between them and then rolled them up in the blanket with the rest of his gear. Zeb rolled the piece of canvas tightly around it. "You sure you can ride?" he said.

"I can ride anything. You ought to see Suba. Wild! Nobody can ride her but me. One day we're gonna race her."

"Suba?"

"Her name is Isuba Lusa, Choctaw for Black Horse. I was only six when I got her. Called her Suba. She's all black. Not another color on her. A beautiful animal."

"Since you're such an expert on horses, you can help me saddle Christmas," he said. "Throw that blanket over him and I'll put the saddle on."

She grabbed the blanket, but even standing on tiptoe, she wasn't tall enough to reach his back. She tried tossing the blanket on, but it kept falling to the ground. Finally, she grasped one corner in each hand and swung the blanket out and over the big horse. Christmas flicked his ears back, turning his head toward her.

Zeb patted her on the shoulder. "Don't worry about the rest," he said. "I'll saddle Christmas."

She let go of the blanket and stepped back. "Don't treat me like a baby," she said in a loud angry whisper. "I always saddle Suba. Never have any trouble. This plow horse of yours is too big for his own good!"

"Suba must be a little Indian pony," he said, with a teasing smile. He picked up the saddle. "This is a real horse."

"Suba is sixteen hands high. She's no *isuba ikitini*. She's no pony!"

He grinned.

"All right," she said, "I have to stand on a box to saddle her and to climb into the saddle. But once I'm on, I can do anything with her. She's the fastest horse alive!"

Zeb loved to hear folks boast about their horses. He never argued with people who thought their horses were faster than Christmas. He just raced them.

Zeb tossed the saddle up on the horse. Hannah stared at it. "What kind of saddle is that?" she asked.

"It's just a standard English saddle, with some additions," he replied as he tightened the girth. "Grampa had the saddle maker add this rifle holster and these straps at the back for the bedroll. These on the sides are for saddlebags. It even has this strap to hold a rope. Grampa has the saddles made up in Nashville. They have what we need for working with horses and for taking long trips."

With the bedroll and rifle in place, Zeb climbed into the saddle. Lifting his foot out of the left stirrup, he leaned over and stretched his hand toward hers. "Put your foot in the stirrup and give me your hand. I'll lift you up."

She swung up easily behind him. Her thin arm circled his waist lightly as if she had ridden this way many times. He walked Christmas slowly, quietly. When they reached the bank above the Natchez Road, Zeb stopped the horse and waited, listening. Satisfied that no one was coming, he urged Christmas forward down onto the dirt road, sunk three feet below the forest floor.

The big horse's front feet skidded down the clay bank, his hind legs bracing against the slide. Zeb expected Hannah to be nervous, but she sat the horse easily and didn't even tighten her arm around his waist.

Huge trees towered overhead, letting in only mottled, filtered light. The narrow road was like a dark, quiet tunnel through the forest.

Zeb spoke in a low voice. "I've never traveled on the Natchez Road before," he said. "But Grampa's told me a lot about it. I think I know where most of the stands are. The Joslin stand should be only about an hour south of here. We'll go there and try to get something to eat. Then we can talk. We'd better keep quiet while we're riding." Hannah tightened her arm around him and muffled a groan against his back as a tree branch whipped against her bare legs. *Probably hurt like the devil against those switch marks,* he thought. *She's been through a lot. Maybe I should take her farther than the first stand.*

They rode without speaking, listening for other riders. Zeb was beginning to hope that this might be an uneventful journey. Suddenly, Hannah's arm tightened around him. She put one hand on his shoulder and lifted up to whisper in his ear, "Somebody's coming." As she spoke, Christmas raised his head and twitched his ears.

Zeb pulled the pistol out of his belt and turned the horse off the trail. He urged Christmas back up the slope and into the forest, thankful that the thick leaf cover on the forest floor would leave no footprints. They made their way deep into the woods. "You've gotta be real quiet, Christmas," he said.

Two horses approached at a fast trot, also going south. Hannah's head turned against his back, following them. After the riders passed, Zeb whispered, "Could you see them?"

"No, I couldn't," she said. "I think I had my eyes closed."

Zeb was about to move the horse back on the road to Natchez when Hannah jabbed a bony finger into his ribs.

Two horses approached at a fast trot, also going south.

"Wait a minute," she whispered. "Why are there men after you? Are they outlaws?"

Zeb shook his head. "No," he said. "Those men don't want me to get to Natchez. They said my grampa was killed by outlaws, but I don't believe it. I'm going down to Natchez to try and find him."

"You traveling all the way to Natchez alone? On the Natchez Road? I don't know anyone crazy enough to do that. They don't call it the Devil's Backbone for nothing."

"*You're* on it alone."

"Yes, but not because I want to be. I know what can happen to people traveling on this road. You've got two men looking for you, and outlaws are hiding in the forest just waiting for people riding alone like you."

"I've gotta do it. When Daddy died of the fever three years ago, I took his place alongside Grampa at the farm. I don't know what I'd do without Grampa. I just feel he's still alive. He may be hurt. He may need me down there."

"If you got people chasing you, how come you're riding this plow horse?"

Zeb had to admit that Christmas was a funny looking horse. He had the big, broad head of a draft horse and the sleeker, muscular body of a race horse. He was bigger than most saddle horses, over seventeen hands high. No horse in Franklin could beat him. But Zeb was glad they still tried.

He turned and looked down at Hannah. "Maybe, one day, when we get to Yowani, we'll race Christmas against Suba."

Hannah snorted. "If we ever get there, you've got a big surprise coming."

Zeb urged the horse forward. As they stepped down onto the narrow trail, he whispered, "I'm gonna keep him at a slow trot. Don't want to overtake anyone. At this hour those two probably won't spend more than a few minutes at the Joslin Stand. Whoever they are, they'll want to make the Gordon Inn by nightfall. That's a full day's ride from here. Most folks goin' south stay there and then take the Gordon Ferry across the Duck River. But we can't take any chances."

"How come you know so much about the Natchez Road if you've never traveled on it?" she whispered.

"Like I told you, Grampa travels on it about twice a year, buying and selling horses in Natchez and even down to New Orleans. Always comes back with stories. I think I know about every inch of it."

They rode in silence. After about an hour, Christmas lifted his head again, his ears pricked forward. Zeb sniffed the air. "I think I smell smoke. The stand must be near here."

He turned the horse to the right off the narrow trail and rode up into the forest. They wound through the trees just out of sight of the road. As soon as he could see the dark walls of the stand, he slipped off the horse and whispered to Hannah, "Sit in the saddle and wait here for me. I'll whistle if everything is all right. Christmas'll come right to me."

Zeb drew the second pistol from the saddle holster and tucked it under his belt. He crept closer, careful not to make a sound. Slowly he pushed a branch down until he could see the door of the stand.

Two horses, wet with sweat, stood in front of the simple log cabin. Zeb recognized them immediately as the horses that Big Red and the Fiddler always rode. The fools hadn't even taken them over to the water trough. The door slammed open. Zeb backed away, allowing the branch to rise slowly into place. Big Red shouted over his shoulder, "Remember, old man. We want that boy dead or alive. Tall, skinny, shaggy-haired boy ridin' a big jug-headed horse. Stole two thousand dollars from McPhee. Stole his prize horse too. You'll get a hundred dollars for his head!"

Zeb gulped. Dead or alive! A hundred dollars for his head! His mouth felt like he was spitting cotton.

The two men mounted and galloped south toward the Gordon Ferry. Zeb slipped quickly back through the trees to where he had left Hannah on Christmas. He stopped and looked around uncertainly. This was surely where he had left her. Hannah was nowhere in sight.

Zeb cursed himself for trusting her. Obviously, she was on her way to Yowani without him. He could whistle loudly and Christmas would come, but so would Big Red and the Fiddler. Zeb kicked at a tree stump, the soft rotten wood crumbling from the blow.

Some dry leaves rustled. Zeb stopped and held his breath, listening. Someone was coming. He ducked behind a tree and watched as a horse came into view. It was Christmas! Hannah sat him as if she had been riding him for years. She had her feet in the straps above the stirrups. He ran toward her, furious with himself and with her. He grabbed the reins. "What was that all about?" he hissed. "Where have you been?"

She leaned over to whisper back. "Christmas was getting restless. He started shuffling his feet. I was sure that he was going to neigh to the other horses. So I took him farther into the forest."

Zeb was still holding the reins. She looked down at him. "You thought I left you, didn't you? I wouldn't do that. I need you.... Who were those men?"

"Tate McPhee's hired hands—Big Red and the Fiddler. Big Red is the craziest and the meanest man I know. Always getting into fights. Usually wins. Only person he's afraid of is Tate McPhee."

"And the Fiddler?"

"He used to be a keelboat fiddler. He has a homemade fiddle —just a cigar box and a stick and four strings."

"A keelboat fiddler?"

"On a keelboat, he would play while the rest of the men rowed, you know, to keep them all together. Got the same pay. That pretty much tells you what the fiddler is like. He's not really violent himself, but he's lazy and'll do anything that Big Red tells him to do."

"And now they're willing to pay a reward for you dead or alive."

"You can see why I'm sure that Grampa is alive. Those men followed me, and they planned to kill me to keep me from getting to Natchez. There has to be a reason."

"They said you're a wanted man."

Zeb shook his head. "I'm *not* a wanted man. But we can't talk about it now." He looked up at Hannah. "I couldn't really blame you if you did take off," he said. "If you stay with me, you're in real danger."

He pointed in the direction of the log stand. "I don't know what to do. Grampa and Joslin have been friends for years, but the old man doesn't know me. He might shoot me on sight."

"We can't stay here, Zeb. Those men will be back when they find out you haven't crossed at the Gordon Ferry."

She slipped her feet out of the stirrup leathers, lifted her bare legs carefully from the saddle, and vaulted to the ground. "We can't even wait and cross at the ferry later," she whispered. "Those men'll tell the ferrymen the same story, probably offer them the same reward."

"We gotta think of something!" he whispered.

"The outlaws I was with never crossed at the ferry, Zeb. Too dangerous. Afraid someone might recognize them."

She looked up into the trees, as if searching for something. "Why don't we go downstream and look for some place where we can ford the river?"

Zeb didn't pause. He climbed up on Christmas and reached out his hand to Hannah. She swung up behind him.

"What makes you think there'll be a place to ford the river?"

Hannah peered into the higher branches of the tall trees. "That's how the outlaws always got across. They'd look for some sign of a trail that leads to the river. There's one at every stand."

Hannah pointed over his shoulder. "Look!" she said. "I thought so. There's the trail. See those blazes that someone has cut on the trees? All we have to do is follow them."

They started down the trail. Zeb turned in the saddle and whispered, "Why are they so secret about the trail?"

"The men who run the stands try to hide their families from the Kaintucks."

When they reached the bottom of the hill, they could see a farm just ahead of them, plowed and planted to corn and oats. Fall and winter vegetables grew in neat rows in a small garden.

The cabin was made of round logs, crudely notched on the ends. Some still had bark on them. The spaces between the logs were chinked with fresh mud, reminding Zeb that the cool weather of fall was just ahead. Colorful skirts and blouses were spread over blackberry bushes to dry.

"Stay out of sight," Hannah whispered. "Those are Chickasaw clothes. If the woman in that house sees us, she'll tell those men where we've gone."

They moved past the cabin into the forest on the narrow farm road.

"Zeb?" Hannah said. She paused as if she were trying to get up her courage to say something.

"Go ahead," he said. "Tell me what you're thinking. You still think I'm an outlaw?"

"Maybe you are," she said. "I don't know."

CHAPTER THREE

The Crossing

Hannah poked Zeb in the ribs.

"Do you hear that?" she asked. "Must be the Duck River. Never heard it so loud."

When they reached the river, Hannah slid off Christmas and ran to the river's edge. "It was never this deep when we crossed it," she shouted over the noise of the rushing water.

She walked along the bank and then made her way back to where Zeb was waiting with Christmas. "Look! See that stone? That was dry a few moments ago and now it's already covered with water. The river is rising and rising fast!"

Zeb looked upriver, shading his eyes. "It's sunny and dry here, but it must have been raining really hard up in the mountains. I don't know whether we can cross it or not."

Hannah looked behind them and back at the river. "I think we'd better cross while we still can. If those men come this way looking for us, we'll have no place to run."

"I don't know," he shouted. "That water may be over Christmas's head. River looks too violent to cross. If one of us slips off, we're done for."

The river was wide, too wide to throw a stone across. The water was the rusty color of the clay banks. Logs and even whole trees rushed past them, sometimes catching on the banks for a moment and then breaking free. The earth they were standing on was damp with the spray and smelled like a freshly plowed field just after a summer shower.

The farm road sloped gently to the water, at the only place on the bank where a horse could wade in easily. Directly across the river they could see the continuation of the road. About a hundred yards downstream, though, the river churned through a narrow gorge ten feet lower than the forest floor. If they were carried too far downstream, it would be impossible for Christmas to get up the steep, slippery bank.

"We've got to try it," Hannah said. She looked out over the raging river and back at Christmas.

Zeb shouted over the roar of the river. "The minute we get into deep water, slip off, swing around me, and grab hold of the mane. You'll float just like you're swimming. We won't be any weight on him and he'll pull us across."

Hannah shook her head slowly, her eyes round and frightened. "What's the matter?"

"I can't swim."

He tilted his hat off his head, the lanyard hanging loosely around his neck and closed his eyes for a moment. *Will I be risking her life if we try to cross here?* he wondered. *Will I be risking both of our lives if I don't try?*

"Hannah," he said finally, "it's up to you. I don't think you'll have a problem. But if you're afraid, we won't cross here."

Hannah nodded. "I think we better cross before it's too late."

"All right. When the horse drops down into deep water, you slip off first, on the downstream side. Grab hold of the mane. I'll hold onto you. You can do it."

Zeb vaulted up on the horse, reaching down to help Hannah mount. She wrapped her arms tightly around his waist and pressed her face hard against his back.

Zeb directed Christmas to the upstream side of the sloping farm road. When he tried to coax Christmas into the water, the big horse balked, sidling along the bank. Zeb shouted back over the noise of the river, "I can't blame him!"

Zeb stroked the horse's neck and talked to him. "You doin' fine boy, jes fine! Ain't nothin' kin skeer you."

He turned back to Hannah. "He won't pay me no mind 'less I speaks Kaintuck. You all right back there?"

Hannah nodded her head against his back. Christmas put one foot and then another in the water, moving out slowly as it got deeper. When the water reached the horse's belly, Christmas lifted his head, struggling to keep his balance. Hannah kept looking behind her. "If those men come along now," she said, "we'll be easy targets."

Suddenly Christmas dropped into deep water. He started swimming, churning his legs fiercely. Only his head and a bit of his upper neck were above the surface now. He snorted with each rapid breath. The water was up to Zeb's waist and almost up to Hannah's shoulders.

Zeb yelled, "Slip off! I'll hold you."

Hannah allowed the water to float her legs up behind her. She struggled to reach around Zeb for the horse's mane, but it slipped through her fingers. Zeb held onto her arm and slid off with her. The force of the water yanked his boots off his feet. He reached down, grabbing a fistful of mane and trying to hold onto Hannah.

Christmas jerked his head away from a floating branch, and Zeb lost his hold. The big horse swam away from them toward the opposite bank. The violent river carried Zeb and Hannah rapidly downstream and away from Christmas.

Zeb's hat, still hanging down his back, filled with water. The lanyard around his neck pulled his head under. He squirmed out of the lanyard and watched the hat spin away downstream.

He felt Hannah slip from his wet fingers. He watched helplessly as she struggled against the current, gasping for air and splashing frantically.

Zeb wasn't sure he could save her. He wasn't that good a swimmer himself. If he tried and failed, they might both drown. Her head disappeared under the water and then came up for a moment, only to go down again. Zeb looked back upstream, but Christmas was nowhere in sight. When he turned back, he couldn't see Hannah anywhere.

Suddenly her head broke the surface, already fifteen feet downstream of him but closer to the other bank. Her black hair was plastered to her head and her face was deathly white. She thrashed around until she caught sight of him, her eyes pleading with him.

Zeb swam toward her as hard as he could, but when she was almost within his reach, her head went under again. He lost any sign of her. Just ahead of him he saw a huge tree lying in the water, twisting in the strong current. It had been uprooted by the flood waters and was clinging by only a few roots to the bank. He prayed that the tree would catch her.

Zeb prayed that the tree would catch her.

Just as Zeb reached the tree, Hannah's head bobbed up again and she slammed against the trunk. She reached out blindly and held on with both arms, coughing up water and sobbing. Zeb inched his way toward her along the tree trunk and grabbed her.

The tree shuddered. Some of the roots broke away from the clay bank.

"Can you get up on the trunk if I give you a boost?" he shouted.

She nodded, but she hardly seemed to have enough strength to hold on against the current.

Zeb began to ease her up on top of the trunk, holding onto the tree with one hand and pushing her up with the other. Her dress was heavy with water. The trunk twisted and turned, tearing at the skin under his arms.

For a moment, the tree lay almost still in the water, as if it were gathering its strength to continue the assault. Hannah grabbed the stub of a branch and pulled herself onto the trunk.

Zeb climbed up behind her. The tree shuddered again as more roots began to tear away from the bank.

"Move, Hannah! Move!" he shouted. "The last roots are gonna go!"

She threw her body forward, wrapping her arms tightly around the trunk. They inched their way toward the bank. The tree twisted violently as more roots snapped. Zeb jumped off into the shallow water upstream of the tree and pulled Hannah with him. Together they struggled up the slippery mud, trying to get away from the huge, twisting mass.

Just as they reached the top of the bank, the last of the roots were torn from the clay with a loud groan. The tree joined the wild current of the river.

Hannah staggered a few feet away from the riverbank until her knees buckled under her. She collapsed, facedown, on the ground.

CHAPTER FOUR

Making Camp

Zeb grabbed hold of Hannah's wrist, yanking her roughly to her feet. "C'mon!" he shouted over the roar of the river. "We've got to find Christmas!"

He started to push through the dense undergrowth and brambles along the river's edge and pulled Hannah, stumbling, behind him. She grabbed hold of his shirt. "Wait!... Wait a minute!" she gasped.

She pointed to the open forest just thirty feet away. "Why don't we go over there? There're no vines or thorny bushes," she said, heading in that direction. "It'll be faster."

Zeb shouted after her, "You go ahead. See if you can get back up to the ford. Can you whistle?"

She nodded.

Zeb turned and began to force his body through the brambles again. He shouted over his shoulder, "I'll keep moving along the bank, watching for Christmas in case he didn't make it."

"If you see him in the water, are you going in after him?"

Zeb looked down at the river just a few feet from where he was standing. The red, muddy water churned against the bank, tearing at the trees and underbrush. Zeb hated to think of Christmas struggling to keep alive.

He had a sudden awful memory of those few seconds when he hadn't been sure he could save Hannah. He had felt so helpless. He wondered if she knew how close he had come to letting her be dragged under for good.

It'd be foolhardy to jump in if Christmas were out of reach, he thought. *But I know I would.*

"Yes," he said, with a lot more assurance than he felt. "I'll probably go in after him. He means a lot to me. I got him into this, and I'll have to try to get him out. You go on now. Run up to the ford. Whistle if you find him."

Hannah slipped into the forest and disappeared. Zeb doubted he would be able to hear her whistle over the noise of the rushing water, but they could cover more ground if they split up. He fought his way through the thick undergrowth, his eyes on the river.

He hadn't gotten far when he heard a high shrill whistle. He pushed through the thicket away from the river and into the open forest. There it was again. He ran as fast as he could through the dead leaves, the ferns whipping against his ankles.

When he reached the clearing, there stood Christmas, knee-deep in golden, late-summer grass, quietly grazing as if nothing had happened. Water still dripped from the muddy and matted mane and tail. His wet, dark-chestnut–colored coat glowed in the late afternoon sun. The big horse raised his head and looked at Zeb, and then lowered it again to pull at the grass.

Zeb waded through the deep grass and threw his arms around the horse's neck. He pressed his face against the warm wet skin. "I thought I lost you, Christmas."

He stroked the horse, running his hands all over Christmas's coat and down each leg to check for cuts or other injuries. As he stood up, he looked around the clearing for Hannah. Then he heard it, a strange sound, almost like the cry of an injured animal.

He walked carefully through the deep grass and found Hannah curled into a ball, with her arms wrapped tightly around her knees. She was sobbing. He knelt down next to her and put his arm around her shoulders. She looked up at him. "I was so scared."

"I know how you feel, Hannah. I was scared too. I really didn't think we would make it."

He looked toward the river. "There's nothing to be afraid of now. Those two men will never be able to cross the ford."

"Do you think they'll give up?"

"Doubt it. They'll go back to the Gordon Ferry, but they'll be at least two days behind us."

She lay down again in her nest of grass. "I'm so tired. Can we rest for a little bit?"

"Good idea. Christmas needs the rest too."

He called Christmas to him and removed the wet packs and saddle, red with river mud. "I know you don't like the hobble, Christmas, but I don't want no Chickasaw a'stealin' you whilst we'uns is restin'."

He hobbled Christmas's forelegs and removed the bridle. He patted the big horse. "Go on and eat, Christmas. Doubt we'll see much grass from here on."

Christmas shuffled a short distance away and began to graze.

Zeb walked round and round in a circle, flattening the tall grass, and then he stretched out on it.

"When we catch our breath, I think we can set up camp in this clearing. I saw the remains of an old campfire over there by those rocks." He glanced over his shoulder. Christmas was pulling at the grass. Zeb closed his eyes. He had never been so tired in his life.

When he awoke, the sun was low in the west. He must have slept an hour or more! Christmas stood looking out toward the river, apparently having eaten his fill for now. Hannah was still asleep.

Zeb rolled over and then stood up very slowly. Every muscle in his body ached. The skin under his arms was scratched and raw. His clothes were damp and cold. He picked up the saddle blanket, still heavy with water and mud, and hung it over a tree branch. He unrolled the canvas from around the bedroll and looked around for some place to put it where it might dry. Hannah opened her eyes and struggled to her feet. "What can I do?" she said.

He looked upriver. The water was still churning as it roared past them. "The way I figure it, we're about five miles west of the Natchez Road. You think there'll be any outlaws or Kaintucks this far off the road?"

"I don't think so. The outlaws want to be close to the road to keep an eye out for travelers. The Kaintucks don't want to get off the Natchez Road."

"Why not? Might be safer for them."

"They don't want to get into Chickasaw territory. The Chickasaw are very violent."

She looked around at the long grass. "Anyone can see the

Chickasaw haven't been here for a while. My guess is that if they do show up, we'll never even see them. They'll probably leave us alone. We're not taking any game or anything."

"In that case, I think we ought to stay here tonight." He held up the canvas sheet. "If we can get a fire going, we might be able to dry these things and maybe even cook something to eat. We can do it after it gets darker so no one will see the smoke."

Hannah headed toward the woods. "I'll look for kindling," she said. "You take care of the wet gear."

As Hannah gathered dry sticks, Zeb kneeled on the ground and sorted through their wet supplies, hoping it would be possible to salvage something. When he lifted the bag of grain, water poured out of the bottom. "This stuff will be all right for Christmas tonight," he mumbled to himself, "but I'll have to leave what he doesn't eat. By tomorrow it will start to rot."

He sat back, cross-legged, lifting the long rifle and balancing it on his knees. When he opened the pan in the flintlock mechanism, he wrinkled his nose at the sharp odor and groaned, "The powder is wet," he muttered, "and I'm sure it's wet in the pistols too."

He cleaned the remaining powder from the pan with his finger. He stood and swung the gun muzzle down, banging with his hand against the barrel. After several tries, the rifle ball slipped from the patch and out the end of the barrel. He put it next to his rifle kit. He poured out the wet powder, cleaned the bore thoroughly, and then ran a greased patch in the bore to prevent rust.

Hannah appeared with an armload of kindling. She dropped the sticks next to the charred logs and stood watching him. Finally she kneeled down and picked up one of the little squares of cloth. "What are these for?" she asked.

"They get wrapped around the rifle ball. Makes a tight fit and keeps the ball snug against the powder."

She turned back into the woods to hunt for more kindling.

Zeb pulled the powder horn out of the saddlebag, glad now that he had double-wrapped it and sealed it in oilskin, a thin piece of deer hide rubbed over and over again with goose grease. He undid one layer and then the other and then lifted the beeswax seal. The powder was damp, but it looked as if it could be dried out. He wondered how long that would take.

Hannah dumped another load of kindling on the ground. She stooped and picked up the tinderbox, groaning with dismay as she opened the cover. She held the box open for him to see. "The tinder is wet," she said, "and the flint and steel are wet too. How're we gonna start a fire?"

Zeb pulled a handful of fine wood shavings out of the box and squeezed it. Soaking wet. He threw the wet tinder away. He wiped the piece of flint and the steel on his shirt. "I don't think water will hurt them," he said. "See if you can find a cedar tree. We can use some of fuzz off the bark. Or look for a bird's nest. That will work too." He pointed to the blackened logs. "Put some of the charcoal from those old fires in with it. That'll make it catch faster."

Zeb watched Hannah as she moved toward the forest to gather the tinder. As tired as she was, she moved lightly, quietly on the balls of her feet. He remembered what his grampa had told him about the Choctaw, who could slip through the forest without making a sound. Hannah was able to do that. *I wonder,* he thought, *if she does that naturally or if she learned it somehow?*

Before she stepped into the woods, Hannah turned and stared at Zeb. "How come you know so much about all this? You could be a Choctaw *nakni,* a brave!"

"Then my grampa could be a Choctaw chief," he said. "He knows a lot about surviving in the forest. Never misses a chance to teach me when we're out hunting. Now I wish I had paid more attention."

When Hannah got back with some cedar bark, Zeb showed her how to shred it and mix it with a little charcoal.

He took the sticks she had gathered and built a little pile of kindling into a small lean-to against one of the partly burned logs. Then he made a nest of the tinder. When he hit the flint against the steel, sparks flew in all directions. The water hadn't affected the flint and steel at all! A spark caught in the cedar-bark tinder. He blew on it gently. In seconds the tinder was aflame. He pushed the burning tinder under the kindling. They had the beginnings of a campfire.

When the fire had burned a while, they took out two of the four potatoes that Zeb had brought from home, wrapped them with sassafras leaves, and then packed them in red mud from the riverbank. Hannah gently pushed the mud-covered potatoes into the hot coals with a piece of kindling.

When the potatoes were done, Hannah pulled them out with a stick, rolling them along the ground away from the fire. They broke the red clay, baked hard around the potatoes, juggling the steaming potatoes in their hands. The skin was black but the inside was white and crumbly. They ate the potatoes, skin and all, grinning at each other.

Full now and warm, Hannah and Zeb stretched out on the ground near the fire and watched the vapor rise from their still-damp clothes.

The stars were clear in the black night, the moon still too low in the east to provide them with any light. Zeb turned on his side to let the fire dry the front of his clothes. Hannah was watching him. There was so much about Hannah that he didn't know. She seemed to know lot about the Choctaw ways of doing things, but she spoke like an educated person. "You go to school in Yowani?" he asked.

"No. When I'm in Yowani, I study with my father or my mother. There are no schools there. When we're in Washington, near Natchez, I go to a friend's house. Her name is Katie McGonnigal. A tutor comes every day for four hours to teach the six of us. Katie's the oldest. She's twelve. I'm the youngest."

Hannah sat up, stretching her arms toward the heat from the fire. "Feels good," she said. "The sleeves are already dry." She tugged at them. "I think they've shrunk some." She looked across the fire at Zeb. "You get to go to school where you live?"

"We don't have school there, either. I used to go up to the preacher in Franklin for grammar and numbers. We were just about to start Latin and Greek, but I had to quit when my daddy died. Grampa needed me at the farm."

"Sounds like you wish you could have a lot more schooling."

"I sure would like to, but there's no way I can. That farm takes at least two people working from before dawn till after dark. We breed and raise horses mostly for the army. My cousins have to come and help sometimes. Mama still rides better than Grampa or me but she can't do much of the really heavy work anymore."

Zeb stretched out, his hands behind his head. He stared up into the black night. "Grampa and Uncle Ira let me read their books.... Maybe someday...."

Suddenly he sat up. "Speaking of books!" he said, jumping to his feet. He lifted a small leather saddlebag from a tree limb where he had hung it up to dry. "I forgot all about this."

He opened the bag and pulled out a package, wiping it against his pants. Then he sat down next to Hannah and carefully unwrapped layer after layer of oilskin, finally revealing two leather-bound books. He fanned the pages, smiling with relief. "Just a little damp," he said. He stood the books open to the air. "Might be dry by morning."

Hannah was lying on her side, watching him. She shook her head in disbelief. "You brought some books to read?"

"Naw," he said. "These are blank books. I hadn't planned to bring them with me. I just never bothered to take this little saddlebag off the horse when I left home."

"What are the books for?"

"My uncle Ira gave them to me. He publishes a weekly newspaper, and he wanted me to have something to write on when I go to the horse auctions and the breeders' meetings."

He reached into the saddlebag. "I have a pencil in here too," he said.

"I've never tried a pencil," she said. "We always used quills." Hannah picked up the pencil and rolled it in her hands. "I would love to be able to write something. I wish I could write about...." She gestured at the forest around them. "About everything...from that first night when I stole your loaf of bread...." She looked down. "I wouldn't really want anybody to read it though."

Zeb handed her one of the books. "I won't have much time for writing now," he said. "You might as well have this one. Go ahead and use it. You can have the pencil too. And don't worry. I'll never read what you write unless you ask me to."

Hannah leafed through the damp pages of the book and then stood it open to dry out. She put the pencil across the top so it would dry too. "Thank you, Zeb," she said.

She lay down again, facing the fire. In moments they were both asleep.

CHAPTER FIVE

Taking Chances

The smell of the woolen blanket, slightly singed by the fire, and the light of the bright morning sun awakened them. The blanket and canvas were dry and so were the clothes on their backs. Hannah's ragged homespun dress was even more lopsided than it had been. The sleeves were short and tight around her arms.

She peered into the forest. "You hear that scream last night?"

"Cougar. Good thing we had a fire."

Christmas was standing near them. Zeb knelt and removed the hobble. He tried to comb the matted mane with his fingers, tugging gently at the tangles. He leaned against the horse, talking quietly with him. "Bet you was wishin' I had the good sense to tote a currycomb."

Hannah burst into laughter. "You could both use one."

Zeb ran his fingers through his hair. He was used to comments about his shaggy head. Didn't bother him. Looked just like his grampa.

"Zeb," she said, "I know you're not an outlaw."

"What made you change your mind?"

"Anyone can see you never stole that horse. That's your horse. Comes when you call him. Besides, if you were an outlaw, you would have left me in the forest. You would have let me drown in that river."

She picked up the tinware pots, looking out over the river that had almost killed them. The water level appeared to be a little bit lower, but trees and other debris were still floating past at high speed. "Wish we could get some water to wash up and to clean the mud off these things," she said. "But I don't want to go near that place."

Zeb tied one of the pots to the end of his rope and walked to the riverbank. Hannah followed, carrying the other pots.

"Zeb," Hannah said, "you never told me why you're traveling down the Natchez Road alone."

"Truth is, there really ain't that much more to tell." He swung the pot down toward the churning river. "I go up to Franklin every week. Uncle Ira lets me help him put out the weekly newspaper. Calls me a printer's devil."

She lifted her head and smiled.

"No reason for your silly grin," he growled. "It's what they call the person who cleans up, puts the type back in the right boxes. I can already set type some, but not fast enough for Uncle Ira."

The pot had hit a pile of brush at the river's edge. Zeb pulled it up and tried again. "Sometimes Uncle Ira lets me write something for the paper. Something I know about, like a horse auction or a horse race."

He tugged on the rope, trying to maneuver the pot into the water. "Day before yesterday when I went into Franklin, I was supposed to go right home, but Uncle Ira had printed some bills about horse trading at the Grady place. I decided to stop by and write a story about who brought what. I knew my uncle would print it if there was room. But anytime there's folks buying and selling, there's always someone who wants to have a bareback race. Nobody can beat Christmas. I didn't get home until dark."

Hannah looked at Christmas as if it were hard to believe that he could win a race. "Your mama doesn't mind your racing?"

"Naw. She's lived and worked with horses all her life. When Grampa and Mama first moved to western Tennessee from the mountains, she was about my age. Worked right alongside him, like I do now. When Daddy died, Mama was out there every day working with Grampa until I was big enough and strong enough to take her place. She still helps with the horses if we're shorthanded."

"What happened when you got home?"

"Tate McPhee was there with his men. He said they'd been stopped by a gang of outlaws. Said the outlaws shot Grampa and stole all the horses."

"But you don't believe it."

"McPhee told Mama and me that Grampa pulled out his pistol and outlaws shot him." Zeb gestured toward their gear. "I've got the only pistols that Grampa owned. You saw me cleaning them. They're nothing but antique dueling pistols."

"So he couldn't have pulled out a pistol."

"That's right. I yelled at McPhee and called him a liar. He got mad. Said we had to be off the farm in a week. He told us it was his farm now that Grampa was dead. He said they had a survivor's agreement. Then he and the men rode up to their cabin."

"Your grandfather and McPhee were partners?"

"No! They just shared the same meadow. They were supposed to help each other at haying time, too, but McPhee's men were always busy with something else. I think Grampa always regretted that he ever met McPhee. There's no way Grampa would make a survivor's agreement with him."

Once again Zeb pulled the empty pot up the side of the riverbank. "Mama said I had to go up and apologize to McPhee. When I got up there near McPhee's cabin, the men were drinking and singing. I heard McPhee shouting at them, 'No more drinking tonight! That boy goes down the Natchez Road looking for his grampa, we got problems!' I turned the horse around and went back to our cabin."

Zeb held onto the rope and lowered the large pot down to the river. This time it floated downstream for a second and then tilted on its side and filled rapidly with water. The force of the river almost yanked the rope out of his hand. He pulled the pot up, and they began the task of filling the other pots. Hannah frowned. "If your grampa can't trust McPhee, why did he travel with him?"

"Grampa was supposed to deliver six horses to the army at Fort Dearborn. He was surprised at the kind of horse the army picked out. They always wanted big strong horses with a lot of endurance and they always came to Franklin to check each horse and to take delivery. But that time they wanted little horses and they wanted them *delivered* to the fort. Grampa didn't want to do it. He said that traveling alone on the Natchez Road with six horses on a lead would be worse than foolhardy."

"And so McPhee and his men offered to go along to help protect the horses?"

"That's right. Grampa hated doing business with McPhee but needed someone to go with him. McPhee said he and his men were going anyway. McPhee wanted to sell some of his sorry horses to settlers going west."

"And when McPhee came back, he said your grandfather had been shot by outlaws and the farm was now his?"

"Yes," said Zeb. "I knew he'd do anything to get the farm. I took Mama to Uncle Ira's house in Franklin where she'd be safe. I didn't tell them what I planned to do. My cousins came out with me to help on the farm. That night, I packed up and headed for the Natchez Road. I left a note for my cousin Josh and one for Mama and another for Uncle Ira."

"You're real close to your grampa."

"Ever since Daddy died of the fever three years ago, I took Daddy's place. Work right alongside of Grampa on the farm. He taught me just about everything I know. I don't know what I would do without him."

"He expecting you to come down to Natchez to look for him, do you think?"

Zeb shook his head. "No, I don't think so. He wouldn't ever let me go with him on his trips down the Natchez Road. He may not be too happy about my going down alone, but I've just gotta do it."

Hannah didn't say anything. The two of them carried the water back to the campsite. They washed off as much mud as they could and began to pack up. After a long silence Zeb admitted, "The truth is, he thinks I take too many fool chances."

"Fool chances?"

"Well, racing bareback up in Franklin, for one thing."

Hannah laughed. "Racing bareback? I race the Choctaw ponies bareback all the time."

Zeb looked down at her. She did ride better than he had expected. Might be fun to race her when they get to Yowani. Maybe he could make a little traveling money from the Choctaws there.

45

Zeb took the saddle off the stump and put it on the ground next to the blanket, getting ready to saddle the horse. "I ride bareback most of the time too. That's how Grampa taught me how to ride. But the races in town are different. Some of the boys think the main object is to pull the others off their horses. A couple of the boys have gotten hurt pretty bad."

"But you still do it?"

Christmas had wandered over into the deep grass. Zeb called him back. He grinned. "Yeah, nobody can even get near to Christmas." He stroked the horse's neck. "He just hates to have another horse in front of him."

He ran his hand up and down the horse's muzzle and over the soft nose. "I was always betting with the boys up in Franklin. Won most of the time." He patted his pocket. "That's where I got the money to make this trip."

"I'd love to take Suba to Franklin one day."

Zeb was sure that if she ever got to Franklin, she would be right out there racing with the boys—if they would let her, which was doubtful.

Zeb rolled the canvas sheet around the bedroll and tied it tightly. "Once I saw a poster for a traveling carnival," he said. "Showed some men riding around standing on the horses' backs. Well, I practiced some on Harlequin, a walking horse we had, and then I challenged those town boys to see who could stay on longest."

"Your grampa didn't like that?"

He shook his head. "Didn't like it at all. I won. Stayed on longest, but I finally fell off. Got a kick in the leg. I limped around for a couple of weeks. Grampa made me work with him anyway, just as if nothing had happened.

"It isn't just that I take chances," he went on. "Grampa hates it when I act like a Kaintuck and let people think that Christmas is nothing but a plow horse. Says it's the same as lying. The way I look at it, if they're trying to take advantage of me, it's all right if I take advantage of them. But Grampa says that if I keep on fooling people all the time, no one will believe me when I want to buy or sell a horse."

"When you make these bets, do you usually win?"

"Almost always. But Grampa doesn't have much use for gambling men. He says if I keep on betting every chance I get, one day someone will goad me into betting my horse, then I'll lose Christmas."

Zeb bridled Christmas and then began to saddle him. He patted the big horse on the neck. *Would I ever be so stupid,* he wondered, *so sure of winning, that I would take a chance on losing Christmas?*

He threw the blanket over the horse, running his hand over his back first to check for burrs or anything else that might chafe under the blanket. He swung the saddle easily onto the horse's back, tightened the girth, and checked the stirrups. Hannah stood behind him, handing him the blanket roll and then the rifle and the pistols.

"I'm surprised," Hannah said, "that he wouldn't let you go to Natchez with him. You're big enough and strong enough to be taken for a man, and you sure know how to take care of this big horse."

Zeb nodded. "I've grown a lot in the last year, but Grampa says that size has little to do with it. He says I'll know when I'm ready."

Hannah looked across the river. "And now you're on the Natchez Road, ready or not, with Tate McPhee's men right behind you." She hunched her shoulders. "If Big Red and the Fiddler are offering a hundred dollars for your head, they're expecting a lot more from McPhee. They'll probably follow you all the way to Natchez."

CHAPTER SIX

Narrow Escape

About midmorning they reached the Natchez Road, and Zeb stopped the horse to listen for travelers. When he was sure no one was coming, he urged Christmas down onto the road and turned south once again.

They arrived at the Sheboss Place in the late afternoon. Zeb left Hannah hiding in the forest with Christmas. He slung his bedroll over his shoulder and moved through the woods toward the road, bending branches back without breaking them. At the road he left a small notch on a tree. He walked to the stand, pretending to be traveling on foot like most of the men on the trail.

The Sheboss Place was little more than a simple lean-to. The only people staying there were three Kaintucks, probably on their way to Nashville and beyond. They paid no attention to Zeb. They seemed more concerned about staking sleeping rights to the tattered and worn bearskins covering part of the dirt floor.

The innkeeper was bent over, stirring something in a huge iron pot hanging over an ember fire in the middle of the room. A hole in the roof over the fire served as a chimney. He looked up as Zeb walked into the shack. "Got no room," he said. "You'll hafta sleep in the forest like the rest." He dipped a big spoon into the pot, lifted it up to sample the rich brown stew, and then poured the contents back into the pot. "I can feed ya. Twenty-five cents for supper and breakfast." He lifted his chin, gesturing toward a rough-hewn table and two benches. "I can feed four at a time, or, if you got somethin' to put it in, you can take it with you."

Zeb sniffed the familiar aroma. He swallowed the sudden rush of saliva in his mouth and pulled a pot from his pack. He looked toward the men arguing about the bearskins and leaned closer to the innkeeper. "You got any grain?"

"Got a horse do ya? Feed'll cost ya twenty-five cents a sack." The innkeeper lowered his voice. "Tell your daddy he better be careful with a horse on the Natchez Road. Plan to sleep with it, his pistol at the ready. Take turns stayin' awake."

The innkeeper nodded toward the three Kaintucks, his voice almost a whisper. "They could just be flatboaters or they could be outlaws. No way of tellin'. Either way, they'd do just about anything to have a horse to ride."

Zeb made his way back up the Natchez Road as quickly as he could with his extra load. When he found the notch he had made, he looked up and down the trail and then slipped into the forest. He watched for the branches he had bent back. Many of them had already begun to return to their normal position. He smiled. He had learned a lot from Hannah.

When Zeb got back to where Hannah was hiding, she was

seated on Christmas holding a three-foot-long tree limb like a club. "What are you going to do with that?" he whispered.

"Just thought I better have something."

Zeb didn't think that the branch would do much good if the outlaws found her.

The next evening they were sitting side by side on a log, well beyond the McLish stand, on the north side of the Buffalo River. Hannah was unusually quiet. Finally she turned toward him. "Zeb," she said. "Do you know what day it is?"

"We've only been gone three days. I left Franklin on the fifth of September. Today must be the eighth."

Hannah turned her head slightly away from him. Tears were running down her cheeks.

"What's the matter? We're making good time. We'll be in Yowani in about two weeks."

"It isn't that," she said. "Today is my birthday. I'm eleven years old."

"Eleven! You don't even look like ten!"

"I know. I haven't grown much lately. But I'm eleven years old today."

"But why are you crying?"

Hannah wiped her hand across her face. "I want to be home, with my family," she sobbed.

Zeb put his arm around her shoulders and thought about how nice it would be to have a little sister like Hannah. She never complained or whined, never seemed too tired to keep moving. But today was her birthday and she was crying.

They left early the next morning and rode south, Hannah riding with the club in one hand. Whenever they heard someone coming, they hurried up off the Natchez Road and into the forest. Zeb worried that Big Red and the Fiddler might be right behind them. But no one ever caught up with them from the north. All of the traffic was from the south, mostly Kaintucks and mostly on foot.

The men they saw traveled in groups, sometimes as many as twenty men walking along the road together. They were usually arguing among themselves or shouting at those in the rear to keep up or be left. It was easy to hear them coming and to get off the road and into the forest.

They had been riding about an hour when a man staggered out of the woods and onto the road. "Help me," he cried. "Been attacked by outlaws!"

Zeb slowed Christmas, but Hannah lifted up behind him. "Go on, Zeb. Go on!" she shouted. "That's an outlaw trick."

Zeb stared for a moment, not sure what to do.

Suddenly the man jumped to the middle of the road and waved his arms, trying to block their way. Zeb squeezed his legs hard against Christmas, and the big horse broke into a gallop, charging directly at the man in the road. The man jumped to one side but reached out and grabbed hold of the stirrup as they passed. Zeb kicked at him, but the man held on. Zeb struggled to pull the pistol out of his belt.

Hannah twisted around and swung the club hard against the man's shoulder. The man dropped the stirrup and fell backward, cursing at them.

Two armed men, mounted on Indian ponies, burst out of the forest onto the trail just behind them. Still clinging to her stick, Hannah tightened her other arm around Zeb's waist. He leaned forward, digging his heels into Christmas. "C'mon boy. Move!"

Two armed men burst out of the forest onto the trail just behind them.

The big horse galloped down the narrow, twisting road. Zeb prayed that Christmas wouldn't step into a hole. The men were right behind them, waving their pistols and shouting, ordering them to stop. They fired at them, but the winding road kept them from getting a clear shot. The men couldn't keep up with Christmas. Finally, they reined in their horses and turned back.

After Zeb and Hannah had galloped another mile down the trail, Zeb slowed Christmas to a walk. He turned the panting horse off the road and up into the forest.

Hannah took a deep breath. She sat back, relaxing her arm. She still held the club as if she were ready to use it. "They're never gonna catch me again."

"Why didn't those two men on horseback come out right away? What were they waiting for?" he asked.

"It's all part of the trap," she explained. "Slow the rider to a walk and he doesn't have a chance."

She patted Christmas on the rump. "I'll never doubt you again, Zeb. I'm sure that Christmas is the fastest horse in Franklin."

CHAPTER SEVEN

The Half-Breed

After the attack by the outlaws, Hannah and Zeb forded the wide but shallow Buffalo River without any difficulty. Three days later they got to the Tennessee River, and there they had no choice. The river was too wide and too deep, and the current was too strong. The only way across was the Colbert Ferry at fifty cents each and fifty cents for the horse. The ferryman wanted to charge them even more for "such a big horse." Zeb was down to twelve dollars.

To make matters worse, a violent thunderstorm forced them to stay that night at the Buzzard's Roost, five miles south of the ferry. The owner said that the inn wouldn't be open for travelers until spring, but they could sleep in the barn with Christmas. In the morning he charged them more than double the usual fare.

As Hannah swung up to sit behind Zeb, he growled, "Let's get out of here."

"What's the matter? Why are you so angry?"

"Oh, I'm sorry. I'm not mad at you," he said, trying to relax in the saddle. "Its the Colbert brothers. George Colbert has the only way to get across the Tennessee River. He has a fancy inn at high prices right there at the ferry. Levy Colbert is building the Buzzard's Roost, the only other place to stay for miles. Grampa says the two brothers are always taking advantage of the poor travelers. They may be important chiefs in the Chickasaw nation, but they're typical half-breeds."

Hannah stiffened and pulled her arm back from around his waist. She held onto the saddle behind her instead. They rode silently for a while. Finally Hannah spoke up, "Zeb, if white men had been running that ferry and those inns, what would you have called them, 'good businessmen'?"

Zeb felt his face turning hot. He hadn't thought of her as a half-breed, but that's what she was. The trouble was, to Zeb and everyone he knew, half-breed didn't just mean someone who was half Indian and half white. A half-breed, they thought, was someone who was untrustworthy, cowardly, greedy, and sneaky. The feeling was that neither the whites nor the Indians could trust them. Hannah didn't fit that image at all.

Zeb sighed. "I'm sorry, Hannah," he said. "That word just slipped out."

Hannah didn't respond.

They rode in silence for the rest of the day. It made the ride seem much longer than usual. That night, while camping next to a stream, Zeb started several times to say something to Hannah, but she just turned away and busied herself.

They sat quietly and ate the last of their provisions. Hannah picked up the pot and the two tin plates, squatting down by the stream to wash them. They usually did that chore together. Zeb knelt next to her and picked up one of the plates, but she snatched it out of his hand and then turned her back on him.

Zeb moved over to the canvas. He felt he had to do something to break the silence. "I bought some dry gunpowder at the Colbert Ferry," he said as if there were no tension between them. "I'll reload the rifle and then I'm going to try to load these pistols. I've never done that before. Don't know how much powder to use."

Hannah kept her back to him.

Zeb finished loading the rifle. When he tried to load one of the pistols, he discovered he had no patch. He wondered if he needed a patch with the pistol. He cut a small square from his shirttail with his knife. Then he poured the powder into the pistol, placed the patch on top of the muzzle, and pushed the ball against the powder with the ram.

Hannah had turned and was watching him.

"Listen, Hannah," he said in a low voice.

She looked away.

Hannah had little reason to trust anyone, but Zeb knew that she had trusted him. He ached, thinking of the pain she must have felt when he made that stupid remark about half-breeds.

He moved quietly to where Hannah was washing the pots. Her body was rigid, waiting. He squatted next to her, letting the water run through his fingers.

"Look, Hannah," he said. "You're right to be angry. I'm sorry I used that word. I don't think any less of you because you're part white and part Choctaw. I'd be happy to have you as my little sister. That's the way I've kinda thought of us as we've traveled together."

She didn't say anything.

"I'd be proud to be a Choctaw. Grampa has more respect for the Choctaw as horsemen and as men of their word than he does for most of the whites we have to deal with."

Hannah looked up at him. "Did you ever call anyone else a half-breed?" she asked in a sad voice.

Zeb hung his head. "No, I never did. It's just the way people talk."

She looked away. "I thought you were different," she whispered.

CHAPTER EIGHT

Mistaken for Outlaws

Two weeks had passed since they crossed the Tennessee River. Zeb hadn't been able to buy any oats or other grain, and it was often difficult to find grass in the forest. Christmas slowed to a walk, his head down. Zeb knew that the big horse couldn't keep up this pace much longer, carrying two riders.

They decided to travel separately for a while, one walking and one riding. Zeb walked and Hannah rode ahead for a mile. With Zeb's knife, she left a blaze on a tree as high as she could reach while sitting on Christmas. She then led the horse deep into the forest and left him tied to a tree. She returned to the road and headed south, carrying her club and ready to run up into the woods if she heard anyone coming.

As he walked, Zeb watched for the blaze. When he found the horse, he rode until he reached Hannah. She handed him the knife, and he continued riding for another mile. There he left a blaze, tied the horse in the forest, and walked on. Hannah was never more than fifteen minutes behind him.

They had been traveling this way most of the morning. It was Zeb's turn to walk. He had just left the horse and started back down the road when he stopped and sniffed the air. Someone was cooking meat! Maybe they would be willing to share. He walked quietly back into the forest along the side of the trail to see who was doing the cooking, outlaws or flatboaters. He hoped he would be able to tell the difference.

Just ahead he could see the smoke and hear the men talking quietly among themselves. He pushed a branch gently aside to observe several men around the campfire. Dressed in homespun pants and shirts, they looked as if they could be flatboaters or farmers coming up the Natchez Road. Kaintucks for sure. One of them stood head and shoulders above the rest. His black hair was plastered to his head with some kind of grease. Black stubble covered his face as if he had only recently decided to grow a beard.

There wasn't a pistol or a rifle in sight. *These men are surely not outlaws,* he thought. He was about to call out to them when he noticed their horses. Six horses saddled and bridled, their lead lines tied to tree branches. Blankets had been thrown over the saddles.

Zeb felt as if some one had punched him in the stomach.

Those were his grampa's horses! He recognized Cleo immediately, jet black with four white stockings and a white blaze down her nose. She had her head over Harlequin's neck. He'd know that piebald anywhere.

There was no doubt about it! Those were the six horses that his grampa had taken to Natchez to sell to the army. Zeb closed his eyes hard and ground his teeth together to keep from groaning out loud. *Tate McPhee had been telling the truth after*

60

all! These men must have killed his grampa and taken the horses. He gulped, rubbing the tears from his eyes. *Grampa dead!*

Zeb wished he hadn't left the rifle with Hannah. He pulled the pistols out of his belt, cocking the flintlocks, ready to fire. Even though he had been able to replace the gunpowder, he wasn't sure that the pistols would work. They might not fire or they might blow up in his hands. He felt so sick thinking about his grampa and what these men had done that he really didn't care. *Thank God,* he thought, *Hannah is a safe distance back on the trail.*

Zeb groaned with pain, thinking about his grampa. The men looked up and Zeb knew that they had heard him. He stepped from behind the tree and held the two pistols out in front of him, pointed at the men. His arms shook. "You there!" he shouted. "You dirty, murdering horse thieves! Put up your hands!"

The four men turned around and raised their hands. They didn't seem to be afraid of him. "I've only got two pistols here," he shouted. "But I can kill two of you before you get me!"

The biggest man of the four looked at Zeb and then looked into the trees behind him. "We unarmed men, sir. We don't got no weapons. We just poor folk, mindin' our own business. Where be the rest of your gang?"

Zeb ignored his question and snarled at him, "I'm gonna hold you murdering thieves till an army patrol comes, and if they don't come, then I'm gonna kill you myself!"

The big black-haired man, who seemed to be in charge, sneered. "Looks like we got us a one-man gang. Don't seem likely, do it?"

Zeb glared at the man. "I know a liar and a thief when I see one. Now, get down on the ground till I figure out what to do with you."

The big man just grinned, looking over Zeb's shoulder. Zeb suddenly realized that there were four men in front of him but six saddled horses! He heard a voice behind him. "Put down those pistols real careful. You make one move and you're dead."

Zeb cursed himself for being such a fool and put the pistols on the ground. All four men lifted their pant legs and took pistols out of leg holsters. The man behind Zeb, joined the others, holding his gun on Zeb and looking around at the forest beyond him. The big man walked over to Zeb and slapped him hard on the face. Zeb fell to the ground. The big man stood over him. "Now who's a liar and a thief?"

Zeb raised himself to his knees. "You are! You murdered my grampa for those horses! You're a yellow-bellied coward!"

The big man smiled. He swung his boot back and kicked Zeb in the stomach. Zeb fell to the ground, doubled over with pain. He started to get up again, knowing that the big man could easily kill him, but it didn't seem to matter anymore.

As he struggled to get his breath, his tear-filled eyes focused on a horse emerging from the woods. There was Christmas being ridden by a man dressed in shabby clothes. He was holding Hannah on the saddle in front of him. Just as the big man was about to kick Zeb again, the man on Christmas said, "Hold it a minute, Sergeant Scruggs. Look what I found!"

All five men turned around. The big man laughed. "What's this, a gang of children?"

The man riding Christmas shook his head. "I don't know. This ragamuffin says she's riding alone." He held up Hannah's club. "She gave me a hard whack with this. Feisty little thing."

Zeb fell to the ground. The big man stood over him.
"Now who's a liar and a thief?"

The big man reached up and yanked Hannah off the horse. "Don't matter none. We'll make short work of the two of 'em 'less they tells us where the rest of the gang be."

Zeb staggered to his feet, holding his stomach. "You cowards!" he shouted. "You kill old men for their horses!"

He looked over at Hannah. She was watching him. She was frightened, but she seemed to believe that he knew what he was doing. After his stupid remark about half-breeds, it was a relief to see that she trusted him. Maybe he could focus their attention on him long enough for her to escape.

The man sitting on Christmas leaned over and looked at Zeb. "Aren't you talking rather brave for someone we're about to hang?"

Zeb spat on the ground. "What difference does it make. You're gonna kill us anyhow."

He looked over at Hannah. "At least let my little sister go. She didn't do anything."

The man on Christmas looked at him and then at Hannah. "Why do you call us murderers and horse thieves? It's our job to mete out summary justice. You know what that means? To find and to punish outlaws on the Natchez Road, without benefit of a trial. We catch them and we hang them."

Zeb shook his head. "That's for the army to do, not for a gang of murderers."

"We *are* the U.S. Army. This is an army patrol, out to catch outlaws like you and bring them to justice."

The big man was standing behind Zeb with his arm loosely around his neck. Zeb shook himself free. The big man reached out to grab him, but the man seated on Christmas raised his hand. "Let's hear what he has to say."

"You call yourselves U.S. Army?" Zeb said with contempt. Anyone can see you're not army."

The man on Christmas leaned back and smiled. "All right," he said. "Show me!"

Zeb knew that it didn't make much difference. Whatever he said, he was sure these men were determined to kill them both. Hannah moved over and stood next to Christmas as if the horse might somehow protect her from these men. Zeb hoped to keep their attention on him. *Run, Hannah,* he thought. *You know how to survive in the forest. You can make it.* He hoped she could read his mind.

Zeb moved over to Harlequin. "In the first place," he said, "if you were army you would take better care of your horses. Look at the mouth on this piebald. You've been using one of those curb bits with the long shanks and the rollers, haven't you?"

The sergeant turned on Zeb as if he wanted to hit him again. "I ride that horse!" he shouted. "It's a worthless nag!" He looked up at the man sitting on Christmas, as if he had explained all of this before. "That animal's gonna need a lot of discipline before it's any use to me." He turned to Zeb, "Besides, the army don't issue nothin' but curb bits. Look, Captain, let us take care of these varmints."

The captain shook his head. "No, Sergeant, let him have his say. I'm interested in what he comes up with."

Zeb ran his hand along the horse's muzzle, pulling the curb bit away from his sore mouth. Harlequin turned his head as Zeb moved to run his hand along the horse's ribs. "You better watch out!" the sergeant jeered. "That horse would rather bite ya than look at ya."

Zeb ignored him. "Spur marks!" he shouted. "You don't need to use sharp spurs on a horse like this one!"

Hannah caught his eye and shook her head. She seemed to be trying to tell him that he was going too far.

Zeb felt he had to keep their attention focused on him. Maybe she would realize what he was doing and slip away. He pulled the blanket off and took a closer look at the saddle. This was a Light Dragoon saddle all right. Hussar-type with the higher pommel and cantle, heavy pads under the seat, and rings for securing equipment. Could these men be army? There was one way to find out. He loosened the girth and put his hands under the saddle blanket. "Saddle sores!" he shouted.

Zeb looked at the men defiantly. "No U.S. Army Light-Dragoons officer would allow a man to ride a horse in that condition."

The captain looked down at the sergeant and nodded.

Zeb turned and looked at the other men. "And these are the sorriest looking men I ever saw. Army! The army doesn't allow mustaches and beards! And look at their gear! We deal with the army all the time. These men wouldn't be accepted as recruits!"

The big man looked as if he was going to hit Zeb again. The captain said, "Hold it, Sergeant. Let's find out some more about our little friends."

He looked down at Zeb. "Why did you call us horse thieves and murderers?" he demanded.

Zeb glared up at him. "These horses all belong to my grampa," he said. "You murdered him! You shot him and stole these horses!"

Zeb hated to let these men see him cry, but he felt tears wind down his face as he thought about what they had done to his grampa.

The captain looked down at Hannah and then at Zeb. "Who is your grampa, boy?" he said in a quiet voice.

Zeb stood as tall as he could. "My grampa's name is Daniel Ryan and I'm Zebulon D'Evereux!" he shouted.

The sergeant stepped forward and grabbed him around the throat. "C'mon, Captain," he said. "Let's take care of these little varmints and get on our way."

"Let him go, Sergeant. It may be that he's telling the truth, but I'm not yet convinced."

Zeb frowned. "I ain't convinced you're U.S. Army."

"I'll prove we're army," the captain said, "and you prove you're Dan Ryan's grandson."

CHAPTER NINE

The Sergeant

The captain turned his head slowly, surveying the group of men and horses. "You're right. We don't look like an army patrol," he said. "If you're Dan Ryan's grandson, you know that the army would never buy horses like these. They aren't big enough or strong enough, and they don't have the endurance we ordinarily need."

Zeb started to say something. The captain held up his hand. "But we don't want to look like an army patrol," he said. "Whenever the patrol is on the Natchez Road, the outlaws all disappear."

The captain looked at Hannah and then back to Zeb. "My name is Captain Paul Morrison. I know 'Cracker' Ryan very well. I've been trading with him for years. Now, prove to me that you two are Dan Ryan's grandchildren."

Hannah spoke up for the first time. "My name," she said in very proper English, "is Hannah McAllister. I am the daughter of Dr. McAllister of Yowani Medical Research Station."

She pointed at Zeb. "He's not really my brother," she said.

"He rescued me from the Mason gang—"

"The Mason gang!" the sergeant shouted. "Mason was killed years ago. There ain't no Mason gang!"

Hannah looked at him quietly for a moment. "You are very much mistaken, Sergeant," she said. "The rest of the gang is still around. They used me for almost six months on the Natchez Road as a decoy."

Zeb noticed a subtle difference in the way the captain looked at her. It must have been the educated way she was talking. She surely didn't sound like an outlaw.

"How did you get away?" the captain asked.

"The night they left for Franklin, they were all busy getting ready to head north. I just disappeared into the forest. They looked for me for a while and then gave up. Kept yelling that they were going to skin me alive if they caught me."

Zeb remembered the swollen switch marks on her legs. Her life with the outlaws must have been terrible.

The captain suddenly showed a lot of interest in what Hannah was saying. "What are they going to do up in Franklin?"

"They were planning a big robbery. Someone's coming down from Nashville with a lot of money."

One of the men gasped, "The army payroll!"

The sergeant looked at the captain and then at the other men. "There ain't no way they could know about that," he said.

Captain Morrison glared at the men. "Only if one of you were talking too much!"

The men stared at the sergeant as if they were expecting him to say something.

The captain turned back to Hannah. "How is it you overheard what they were planning?"

"They told me I had to be the decoy for it."

"When were they expecting the money?"

"Between October seventh and tenth."

"We better get moving, Sergeant. Looks like they're going to need us up north."

The men immediately began to collect their gear. Zeb was finally convinced that they must be army—they moved so quickly and so quietly, each man with a job to do.

"Sergeant," the captain said, "no point in trying to look like Kaintucks. Have the men pack for forced march. We're not going to try to fool anybody."

Four of the men slipped into the woods while the other two kept their pistols pointed at Hannah and Zeb. The four returned with six rifles.

Then two of the men ran into the woods. One returned carrying saddle holsters with bearskin covers and tubular leather valises. The end of each valise was marked with the initials USLD. The other man came back to the clearing, carrying six sabers in their scabbards.

"All right," Zeb said. "I can see that you're army. USLD—that stands for U.S. Light Dragoons. But it's not because of all the equipment. You could have stolen that from some army patrol."

The captain smiled. "What then?" he said.

"It's the way you're doing things. That's how the army acts when they come to the farm to pick up the horses. Everybody has a job to do, and it's all done as if you've done it many times."

The captain looked down at Zeb. "You know a lot about the mounted Light Dragoons, but I'm still not sure about you," he said.

The sergeant interrupted. "He's probably one of those deserters. That's why he knows so much. We can hang him now, or take him to the army post and hang him there."

The captain looked from Zeb to Harlequin and smiled. "Tell you what. Cracker Ryan used to boast all the time about his grandson Zeb's ability to ride. Thought he might be good for the mounted Light Dragoons some day. Why don't you show the sergeant here how to ride that horse?"

The sergeant grinned. "That'll be a good one. That crazy horse'll probably kill him."

The other men were already rolling their blankets into tight bedrolls. They stopped to watch Zeb work with Harlequin.

Zeb turned his back on the sergeant and began to talk to Harlequin. They knew each other well. Zeb had ridden him every day until Christmas was old enough to ride. Harlequin was a joker. Grampa said he was the only horse he knew that had a sense of humor. But Zeb knew how to ride him. He was a walking horse. Never could be made to gallop for long. But he had a very fast walking gait.

Zeb put the saddle on the ground and the saddle blanket on top of it. He gently rubbed Harlequin's back. Unhooking the reins from the curb bit, he connected them at the snaffle. The sergeant jeered. "You gonna ride bareback and no curb bit? You do that," he said, "and you won't last five minutes."

Zeb couldn't resist. "You want to make a small wager, Sergeant?" he said. "What kind of odds will you give me?"

The sergeant reached into his pocket and pulled out a coin. "My golden eagle to your half eagle or five silver dollars if ya got 'em."

Zeb looked at him and shook his head. "I have a better deal for you. I'll bet my two pistols, the rifle, all the provisions, and the ten dollars I have left. If I can't stay on for more than five minutes you get 'em all. If I can, I get to keep the horse for Hannah to ride."

The sergeant sneered at Zeb. "You're a bigger fool than you look, boy. That girl'll never be able to ride that horse. I thought ya knew a lot about the army. We can't sell our horses, much less bet 'em. Besides, why should I bet my horse against that pitiful pile of provisions?" The sergeant looked at Christmas. "Now if you want to bet your horse...."

Zeb shook his head. "You're the one who doesn't think I can stay on, Sergeant."

The other men stood behind the sergeant, arguing among themselves. Finally one of them stepped forward. "Go ahead," he said to the sergeant. "If Mike Scruggs can't ride that crazy horse, nobody can."

The sergeant looked at the men as if he weren't sure that they were sincere. When he turned back to the captain, one of the men elbowed the man next to him. They both grinned. Zeb was sure of it. These men were hoping that the sergeant would lose!

The captain shouted, "You men! Get those horses ready and police this campsite! We'll be leaving here this afternoon!"

He turned to the sergeant and said, "If you want my advice, Sergeant, don't take the bet. If this really is Zebulon D'Evereux, he probably can ride that horse. His grandfather says he can ride anything. If you want to take his wager, you can do it, but against my advice."

"But I can't bet an army horse."

"These are not officially army horses. They're not branded. If you lose, however, you will have to replace the horse."

The sergeant seemed a little less sure of himself. But Zeb wasn't a horse trader's grandson for nothing. He smiled as if he were sorry for the sergeant. "Course," he said, "if what you were saying was just a lot of wind.... Maybe you don't know how to ride as well as you thought."

The men stopped what they were doing to watch the sergeant's reaction.

The sergeant glared at Zeb. "I'll take the wager!" he hissed. "That horse against all of your provisions, your pistols, and the rifle.... And throw in your saddle, too. The wager is that you can't stay on for more than five minutes!"

The sergeant already had Zeb's two pistols in his belt. The saddle wouldn't make much difference if he lost the bet. He suddenly had second thoughts. If he lost, he and Hannah would be traveling with no gear at all, no protection. He wished he could withdraw the bet—or at least part of it. Harlequin was always unpredictable. He had ridden the horse every day for more than a year, and every day it was a battle until the horse decided to give up and behave. Maybe Grampa was right. He took too many chances. He looked up to see Hannah watching him. She seemed very confident. He shrugged. "Done!" he said.

Zeb turned back to the horse and began to talk to him quietly. The sergeant snorted. "He talks to horses like a Choctaw. He'll be great in the U.S. Army."

Zeb ignored him. He continued to talk in a low voice while stroking Harlequin's muzzle. He moved his hand slowly down the horse's neck to the withers. Just as he expected, Harlequin jumped sideways, kicking out a hind foot and skittering forward. Zeb held onto the reins as the horse made a circle around him.

The sergeant was laughing at him. "What's the matter, boy? You afraid of that horse?"

Zeb put his left hand on the horse's back. Harlequin was so much smaller than Christmas, mounting was going to be easy. Staying on might be the problem, though. It was hard to know what the poor horse had been through with the sergeant.

He pressed down with his left hand. As the horse shifted and began to move forward, Zeb vaulted on.

The little horse tried all of his usual tricks, jumping sideways, bucking, and twisting. He ran as close to a tree as he could and tried to scrape Zeb off. His choppy and irregular gait kept Zeb bouncing on his back. Zeb just chuckled and relaxed. He talked quietly to him. "Thatta boy. Good boy. What a clown you are!"

The little horse decided to behave. Zeb could feel Harlequin's muscles relax. He squeezed his knees, to let Harlequin know he was in charge, and then Zeb walked him quickly around the clearing. Harlequin lengthened his pace, picking up his feet. Zeb sat erect, his hands soft, his only movement a slight twisting of his hips, matching the horse's rhythm. He lengthened Harlequin's stride some more around the clearing, relaxing the horse and encouraging Harlequin to trust him. When Zeb felt confident that the horse was at ease and compliant, he turned Harlequin toward the sergeant. The sergeant stepped back and pulled one of the pistols from his belt. Hannah gasped.

"Sergeant! No!" the captain shouted.

The sergeant ignored the captain's order. He didn't aim at Zeb. He raised the pistol high in the air, pointing toward the sky. Zeb knew what he was trying to do. The sergeant was going to try to spook Harlequin. But Harlequin had been raised with army horses. He had heard gunfire every day of his life. It was part of the schooling that the horses were put through.

"Don't shoot!" Zeb yelled. "That pistol ain't safe!"

The sergeant smirked at him and fired the pistol. There was a tremendous explosion, much louder than Zeb had expected. The sergeant screamed, dropping the pistol to the ground. He bent over, holding onto his hand. It was black.

"You fool!" the sergeant groaned. "You put twice too much powder in that pistol."

Zeb rode over to the captain. "Is the five minutes up, sir?"

The captain was glaring at the sergeant. Without turning his head, he nodded and Zeb vaulted off the horse. He led the horse over to Hannah and said, "This horse is yours now, Hannah. Let me give you a leg up."

Hannah looked at Zeb, her eyes wide with surprise. "Now?"

Zeb nodded.

Hannah grasped Harlequin's reins in her left hand and stroked his neck with her right, talking to him in a low voice. Zeb helped her up.

The little horse danced around, but Hannah sat him well, moving easily with his twisting and turning. Harlequin soon settled down. When she squeezed her legs against his flanks, he stepped out around the clearing.

The sergeant held onto his injured hand, groaning with pain. "The whole thing is a trick!" he shouted. "These outlaws on the Natchez Road have a hundred ways to take advantage of people." He turned to the captain. "He never proved he was old man Ryan's grandson!"

There was a tremendous explosion.

The captain paused and then spoke to the sergeant in a low voice. "I will deal with you later, Sergeant Scruggs. I do not allow my orders to be disobeyed!"

The captain mounted his own horse, and Zeb climbed up on Christmas. Zeb walked his horse over to the sergeant. "I'll take those pistols back, Sergeant," he said.

The sergeant was still supporting his burned hand with the other. He grimaced as he let it go. He pulled the one pistol out of his belt with his left hand, handing it to Zeb muzzle first. Then he picked up the second pistol from where it lay on the ground. He stood close to Zeb, handing him the pistol with the muzzle pointed at Zeb's chest.

When Zeb leaned down and grabbed the still-hot barrel, the sergeant held onto it, drawing Zeb closer to him. "You and me will meet again, boy," he growled. "And when we do, you'll wish you had never tried to make a fool of me in front of my men."

Pigeon Roost

C aptain Morrison watched as the sergeant stalked off. "Tell me about your grandfather," he said to Zeb. "What makes you think someone stole his horses?"

Zeb told him everything that McPhee had said when he came back to the farm.

"That man's a liar!" the captain shouted angrily. "We bought these horses from your grandfather in Fort Dearborn about a month ago. We paid him in cash."

Excited, Zeb moved Christmas closer to the captain. "You saw him?" he asked. "He was all right?"

"He was fine. He's a hard man to put down. They don't call him 'Cracker' Ryan for nothing. Not many men can get the best of him when he has that whip in his hand."

"I've even seen him kill a big rattler with his whip," said Zeb. "He doesn't believe in killing things, but the rattler was coiled, ready to strike one of the horses. But what good's a whip against four armed men?"

The captain shook his head. "I don't know, Zeb. I've heard some amazing stories about your grandfather and that whip."

Zeb was now even more eager to leave. "We better be on our way, sir. We hope to reach Yowani tonight."

"You'll never make it tonight, Zeb. You're at Line Creek. Yowani is a full-day's hard ride from here."

The captain moved his horse next to Hannah and Harlequin. He pulled her wooden club from a strap on his saddle. "Miss Hannah," he said. "You'll want this back. You're pretty good with it." He turned and pointed to the smoky campfire. "Why don't you two take some of those birds with you?" Zeb recalled that the smell of meat cooking was what originally had attracted him to the army camp. Now for the first time, Zeb turned to look at the fire. He was surprised to see that they were cooking pigeons. A pile of more than a hundred birds was stacked near the fire and at least a dozen were still roasting on skewers. "What are you doing with so many pigeons?" he said. "You can't possibly eat 'em all."

"You're right," the captain said. "We can't. We roast these birds to lure the outlaws. Make them think we're just unarmed Kaintucks traveling north from the flatboats. If they come and just ask to share the meat, we give it to them. If they try to hold us up, they discover that we're really armed. Then, it's summary justice."

He pointed to the birds on skewers. "We've already eaten all we want. Go ahead and take what you can carry."

Zeb still could not understand. "But why did you kill so many? It must've cost a fortune in powder and ball. I can't see killing what you ain't gonna eat."

The sergeant, still holding his burned hand, broke in. "He sounds like one of those ignorant Choctaws. If he don't want these birds, we'll just leave 'em for somebody else."

"Sergeant Scruggs!" snapped the captain. "I will talk with you before we break camp."

The captain turned to Zeb. "You'll understand why we killed so many when you travel another couple of hours down the Natchez Road. At this time of year, hundreds of thousands of them are in the trees. They call them passenger pigeons. If you use bird shot, one shot will bring down a dozen. There are more birds than anyone will ever use."

Zeb dismounted and picked up two of the skewers hanging over the coals, two large birds on each one. Handing both skewers to Hannah, he remounted and rode up alongside her. He took one skewer in his free hand.

As they turned the horses to ride south down the trail once more, they could hear Captain Morrison issuing orders. "Return to the fort, Sergeant Scruggs. You are no use to me with that hand, and you are no use to me if you cannot obey a direct order. If you want to buy a horse in Yowani, that is up to you, but you will use your own funds. No army reimbursement. You will also replace the cost of that horse."

The sergeant began to say something, but the captain interrupted. "No, Sergeant, we will not discuss it now. Remember also that you are responsible for that saddle. You will have to carry it until you can arrange for a mount. That is all, Sergeant!"

Zeb and Hannah kept the horses at a walk until they were out of sight of the camp. It was impossible to move at a faster gait holding the skewered pigeons. Zeb motioned to Hannah to stop. "We've got to find a better way. We'll never make time this way, and I don't want to meet up with the sergeant in Yowani."

Hannah turned toward him, and Zeb sensed that she wanted to say something but was reluctant to say it. "Go ahead," he muttered. "You're right. I shouldn't have made an enemy of him."

Hannah shook her head. "No," she said. "I don't think you could have done anything to avoid it, unless you had fallen off Harlequin before the five minutes were up."

Hannah looked at him shyly. "What I wanted to say, Zeb, is that you were very brave back there. I was so scared.... You were trying to keep their attention so I could slip away, weren't you? But I couldn't have left you there...." She turned her head away.

She sighed and changed the subject. "Why don't we put these pigeons in the cook pots and wrap them back up in the bedroll? That'll keep 'em warm, and we'll be able to make time."

They packed the pigeons, licking their fingers as they covered the pots. They longed to stop and eat, but it was too risky with the sergeant right behind them. Hannah rode just ahead. Zeb was able to move Christmas into a comfortable pace that nearly matched Harlequin's fast walk. Hannah turned and smiled at Zeb. "This is like riding a rocking horse."

In places the trail was wide enough to ride side by side. "Hannah," Zeb said, "you ride better than anyone your age I know. Bareback too! Where'd you learn?"

"I used to spend all of my time with the other children at the Choctaw villages. We rode bareback every day with a leather noose over the horse's muzzle. Then Father bought Suba for me and I learned how to ride with a saddle and bit."

They had traveled for a while, when Hannah raised her hand. Putting her finger up to her lips, she motioned to Zeb to stop and listen. Zeb heard a noise unlike anything he had ever heard before. They walked the horses slowly forward, ready to turn around and gallop away from the first sign of danger.

Christmas was prancing sideways and snorting, something he often did before a race.

Hannah sat back and looked up, staring at the trees. She signaled Zeb and pointed up over her head. The trees were filled with pigeons! Hundreds of thousands of pigeons! The branches of the big trees were bent with the weight of the birds, their bodies blocking out the sun.

Zeb felt a wet drop on his cheek, another on the back of his hand. Bird droppings! He urged his horse forward. "Come on!" he shouted. "Let's get out of here."

They rode for almost an hour before they were beyond the pigeon's roosting place. Hannah stopped at the first creek they saw, hopping off Harlequin to wash her face and rinse out her hair. She stood up and patted Harlequin. "We're going to have to wash the horses when we stop tonight."

A few pigeons rested in the trees not far from where they had stopped. Hannah stood still and looked at them more closely. "Beautiful bird," she whispered. "Almost pink. Long tail and blue-gray head. Much bigger than the pigeons in Natchez."

Hannah looked around again as if suddenly recognizing something. Zeb was about to laugh at her wet face, until he saw that they were tears running down her cheeks. "I know about this place," she said. "The Choctaw call it *Pachanusi,* The Place Where the Pigeons Sleep—The Pigeon Roost."

"Why are you crying?"

"We are so close to my home," she said, wiping the tears from her face with the back of her hand. "I've been trying not to think about my mother and father. I was sure that I would never see them again. Now they are only a day's ride away. I just can't wait to see them."

Hannah stood still and looked at the pigeons more closely.

They rode on, stopping only when the sky began to turn red with the setting sun. They camped in a little clearing well off the road. Zeb took the saddle and packs off Christmas, hobbled both horses, and let them graze. He spread out the canvas and the blankets and, finally, he and Hannah were able to eat the pigeons.

As soon as Hannah finished eating, she licked the fat from her fingers and then took the diary out of Zeb's saddlebag. She made a quick sketch of the pigeons, and then she began to write in her diary. She had been doing that every night since the Duck River. Zeb wondered what she could be writing, but he remembered his promise never to look at what she wrote unless she asked him to.

He looked over at Hannah. She was almost home and he was more than halfway to Natchez and his grampa. Somehow, though, he felt a little sad.

He unfolded the saddle blanket and stretched out on it, his head resting on his hands. He looked up through the trees at the evening sky. "Grampa would never have killed all those pigeons," he said. "Captain Morrison says they will never run out, but if everybody kills as many as the captain and his men did, someday there won't be any left."

CHAPTER ELEVEN

The Walking Wolf

The narrow trail to Natchez had become much broader, wide enough now for a team and wagon. Zeb and Hannah passed open meadows and even fenced fields, definite signs that people lived along this part of the Natchez Road. Hannah had Harlequin moving as fast as he could go. She kept looking back at Zeb.

She turned the horse to go through a gated entrance and then pulled him to a sudden halt. The gate was closed.

When Zeb came alongside, she motioned toward the buildings, but she wasn't saying anything.

Zeb was about to dismount and open the gate when an old Choctaw carrying a musket galloped toward them. He wore the tattered and worn homespun clothes of a white farmer. The horse, a sleek bay, moved easily. The Indian swung the musket until it pointed at Zeb. "Stay on your horse!" he demanded.

He looked at the two of them, and then looked up and down the Natchez Road behind them. "Who are you, and what do you want?"

Harlequin danced around, but Hannah pulled him up alongside the gate. Hannah leaned toward the old man. "Isushi, is that you? I've never seen you without your deerskin coat. It's me, Hannah!"

The Indian winced. He swung his head quickly, checking the Natchez Road again.

Hannah cried out, "Isushi, don't you know me? You used to help me get up on my horse. Isushi! Don't you remember? It's Hannah!"

She touched the horse with her heel. She turned so that she was facing Zeb. "Isushi taught me to ride and how to hide in the forest. His name is Choctaw for fawn—a deer so young, he still has his spots. No one can see him in the forest."

Isushi stared at her face. Suddenly, he sat back on the horse and shouted, "Hannah! It is you! Where have you been? What happened to you?"

Hannah hung her head and spoke to him in Choctaw.

The Indian glared at Zeb and then looked at Hannah carefully. "Are you all right, Hannah?" he asked. "Not hurt?"

Hannah nodded, "I'm all right, Isushi." She pointed her chin at Zeb. "That's Zeb. He saved me from the Mason gang. He is almost as fearless as a Choctaw warrior."

The old man looked at Zeb again and then turned and stared at Hannah.

"Isushi, it's so good to see you," she said. "Will you open the gate? I am anxious to see my mother and father."

The old man shook his head. "Your mama and papa are not here anymore, Hannah."

"What happened to them?" she cried, her horse startling at the sudden noise.

The old man held up his hand. "They're all right, far as I know, Hannah. They waited three months for news, hoping that someone was holding you for ransom. But they didn't hear anything at all. They moved back to Washington."

Hannah sagged against Harlequin's neck. "But I was so hoping to see them today," she despaired.

"You can stay at the Yowani Council House," the old man said. He pointed toward the cluster of buildings behind the gates. The one near the entrance was built like a farmhouse; it was covered with cedar shakes, weathered pewter-gray. The others were made of sawed logs. "No one is allowed in the Research Center grounds right now," the old man said. "There is no more medical research here."

They rode down the Natchez Road about a mile to a log cabin in the center of a clearing. Hannah rode slumped over, letting the other horses lead. The three of them dismounted and led the animals to the water trough near the simple, open stables almost hidden behind the cabin.

Hannah walked Harlequin into a paddock. She took off his bridle and rubbed his neck. After throwing some hay in a feeder for him, she hung up the bridle and then went to the trough to wash her face.

Zeb knew that she was terribly disappointed. Her parents were probably alive, and she had reached Yowani and was safe with people she knew, but there was still a long, dangerous trip between Yowani and Washington. *She probably wonders if she'll ever see her parents again,* he thought.

Zeb led Christmas into the paddock with Harlequin. He spoke quietly as he removed the bedroll, the saddle and blanket, and then the bridle. "Get some rest tonight, Christmas. I'll see that you get a good ration tonight and tomorrow. We may not see much more than grass from here to Natchez."

Isushi was watching him, as if he still weren't sure of him. "Did you learn that from a Choctaw brave?" he said. "Only the Choctaw talk that way with horses. I have never seen a white man do it."

Zeb nodded. "My grampa does. He might have learned it from some of his Choctaw friends, though. Just seems natural, that's all."

Zeb patted Christmas, and he and Isushi walked around the council house to the entrance. A tall Choctaw, not much older than Zeb, opened the door. He stepped back. He seemed surprised to see them. He looked first at Isushi and then at Zeb. "Who is this?" he growled to Isushi. "Why did you bring a white man to the council house?"

"His name is Zeb. He saved Hannah's life. He rides like a brave. I knew you would want me to bring him here."

"Hannah is home?" he cried.

"Yes. She is all right, not hurt. She is cleaning up."

The young brave eyed Zeb warily and then stood with his arms outstretched as if to hug Zeb. He seemed to guess that Zeb was unsure of what to do. He dropped his arms and stuck out his hand and took Zeb's in his. "Choctaw braves do not normally shake hands; we hug."

"His name," Isushi said, turning to Zeb, "is *Nashoba Nowa,* The Walking Wolf. Everybody calls him Nashoba."

"Sorry about the formal introductions," Nashoba said. "Among the Choctaw, it is wrong for a warrior to tell another his name. Someone else must do it."

He dropped Zeb's hand. "Tell me about Hannah."

"She's at the horse trough, washing her face. She's—"

Nashoba leaped off the porch and started around the building. Isushi and Zeb followed close behind him. "Hannah!" he shouted. "You're back! You're safe!"

Hannah turned just as Nashoba reached her. He picked her up and swung her around. Hannah screamed, "Nashoba! Nashoba! I thought I'd never see you again."

They switched from English to Choctaw and back to English, both talking at the same time. Hannah was smiling again.

The four of them walked around the building, Nashoba and Hannah talking and laughing. Hannah ran up the steps to the council house porch. She suddenly stopped and turned, looking down at the three of them. Her face turned red. "I'm sorry," she said. "Nashoba, this is Zebulon D'Evereux. He saved me from the Mason gang, he—"

Zeb interrupted. "Hannah escaped from the Mason gang by herself. We've been traveling together since Franklin."

Nashoba climbed the steps and opened the door, motioning for them to go into the council house. Zeb stopped at the door. His grampa had told him how important the council house was to the Choctaws. Whites were usually allowed to enter only when there was a treaty to be discussed. Nashoba called from inside the building, "Come in! Come in! You are welcome here."

Zeb stepped inside and looked around. It was just one large room. Two small openings served as windows.

Nashoba stood in the sunny part of the room next to one of the windows. Hannah stared at him. "Nashoba," she said. "Why are you wearing worn-out homespun pants and that old deerskin jacket?"

Nashoba looked over at Isushi as if he wondered how much to tell her. "We had a very bad sickness here, Hannah. Many people died. Since your father left, we didn't have anyone to tell us what it was. The *Alikchi,* the head medicine man, closed the station and then told us to burn all of our clothes and blankets. He said that is what your father would have done."

Nashoba looked down at his clothes. "I pulled these out of the throwaway box. Your father left behind a box of outgrown clothes discarded by the staff of the Medical Research Center. He always kept the clothes until he found someone who needed them."

He pointed to the old Choctaw. "Isushi and I have been trying to guard the Research Center from the Kaintucks and the outlaws. For a while it was impossible. We lost almost all of the horses and most of the special cattle your father brought here. But now that word has spread about the sickness, we aren't bothered much."

Hannah grabbed his arm. "Suba! They took Suba?"

Nashoba shook his head. "No, your father and mother took four horses, including Suba and a packhorse loaded with laboratory equipment. They went back with an army patrol."

Zeb looked around the room once again. No furniture except for a simple table and chair next to one of the windows. One of the walls had a number of shelves filled with books. A book was open on the table. Nashoba apparently had been reading when they arrived. Nashoba went over to the table, slipped a long feather in the open pages, and then closed it.

"Do you read?" Nashoba asked. When Zeb nodded, Nashoba waved at the books on the shelves. "I have read all of those on that side. Now I am reading John Locke and Jean Jacques Rousseau on the natural rights of man." He picked up the book he had been reading. "This book also contains the

Constitution of the United States and the Declaration of Independence. 'We hold these truths to be self evident,' he quoted, 'that all men are created equal, that they are endowed by their Creator with certain unalienable rights, that among these are life, liberty and the pursuit of happiness....'"

Zeb didn't know what to say. The Indians were not treated as "equals." He wondered if they ever would be. He moved toward the bookshelves. "You've done a lot of interesting reading. I envy you these books."

Nashoba looked at him for a moment. "Thank you," he said. "You are welcome to read any of them while you are here."

"I'm surprised you have so many."

Nashoba said in a quiet voice, "I have applied for admission to Dartmouth College, in New England."

"Admission to college? Where did you go to school?

Nashoba smiled at Zeb's enthusiasm. "I studied with my father whenever he was here. He spent part of every year with us. He always came with a saddlebag full of books for me."

"And now he has brought you books to get you ready for college?"

"No. He was unable to come. He's visiting the Creeks. He expects to meet with Tecumseh and Tecumseh's brother, the Prophet. His friends at Dartmouth College sent a package of books with a note saying that they will continue his commitment to me."

"Does he work at Dartmouth?"

Nashoba nodded. "He is doing research among the People, learning the various languages and keeping detailed information on the similarities and the differences in the music, the dances, the games, the ceremonies, the religions, even the food."

"The People?"

"Yes, the People, the *Okla*. That is what we call the various Nations: the Chickasaw, the Creek, the Cherokee from around here; and the Shawnee, the Iroquois, and others from the north. We don't use the word *Indian*."

He put the book back on the table. "If attending Dartmouth is not possible, I shall apply for admission to a new school, Jefferson College, in Washington. That is less than two hours easy riding from Natchez, about a week to ten days from here."

Nashoba turned to face Zeb. "Speaking of clothes, you may want to see if you can find something in the throwaway box."

Zeb looked down at his pants. They were short, but they didn't look too bad.

Nashoba smiled. "Maybe nobody told you that the seam is out in the back. You're just too big for those pants."

Zeb reached around and felt the torn seam. When he glared at Hannah, she giggled. "What good would it have done to tell you?" she asked.

Nashoba pointed to a huge wooden box in the corner of the room. "We moved all of the safe clothes in here. Pick out what you need, and then Isushi will show you a spot in the creek where you can wash."

Zeb tilted the heavy lid of the box against the wall and began to sort through the clothes, holding some of them against his body for size. He dropped the clothes that were too small for him on the wooden floor.

Nashoba pulled out a pair of pants and a shirt. "Hannah," he said, "you ought to pick out some clothes, too. That dress you're wearing is worn out. Boys' clothes might be best." He held them up for her to see. "These were all dyed with butternuts, the color of dead leaves. Wearing these you can travel in the forest and not be seen."

With his new clothes slung over his arm, Zeb walked with Isushi to the barn. There Zeb opened the bedroll and took out the small bar of lye soap. It hadn't been used very much. They walked a short distance from the council house on a well-worn path to a bend in the creek. The water was deep and clear and slow moving.

Zeb took off his clothes and jumped in. He swam from one side to the other and then stood in the shallow part and rubbed the bar of soap all over his body, wrinkling his nose at the strong odor. His skin tingled. He washed his hair and rinsed, and then started washing all over again. He had thought he would never be clean again!

Isushi shook his head. "You are a lot like Nashoba. He never wants to get out of the water. It is time to go back now. Come!"

Zeb climbed out and tried on the clothes he had found in the box: homespun pants, a shirt, and a deerskin jacket. They were worn, but they fit.

When Zeb and Isushi got back to the council house, Nashoba said, "Isushi will go over to the village and let them know that we have two more to feed. The women will bring the food to us in about an hour. You two can stay here as long as you like."

Zeb was hungry, but he was anxious to get moving. "We really can't stay here very long. Just tonight. There are some people looking for me. I've got to try to keep ahead of them. You say it's about a week to Natchez?"

Nashoba nodded. "It's a week if you can ride eight to ten hours a day."

"That's going to be rough. Maybe it would be better if Hannah stays here with you. She can wait for the next army patrol."

"I'm sure she expects to go with you. She can handle a lot, as you know. The big problem won't be the hard riding. The road to Natchez is still a very dangerous road to travel."

"That's what worries me, especially if Hannah—"

"Look, why don't I go with you?" Nashoba broke in. "The village will send someone else out here to help guard the Research Center. I have something very important to do at Yockanookani Village, and it's on our way."

CHAPTER TWELVE

Brave Horse

The three of them left the Choctaw village the next morning, moving at a quick trot, hoping to make Choteau's Inn by nightfall. Nashoba led them on Choctaw trails as much as possible. When they did have to use the Natchez Road, they moved off if they heard someone coming.

It was a long day's ride—a full thirty miles—before they found Choteau's Inn. Fortunately they had been able to stop every hour or two to water the horses. Even so, the horses and riders were very tired when they arrived.

Before they settled in for the night, Nashoba disappeared for a while and returned looking very serious. He was unusually quiet, but every once in a while he would chuckle to himself. Zeb looked over at Hannah, who shrugged as if his strange behavior was nothing to be concerned about.

The next morning, Nashoba told them that the Norton Inn was only twelve miles away, half a day's ride, but Brashear's Inn, the one after that, was more than fifty miles down the road.

"There is another choice," he said. "We can see if we can stay at a Choctaw village that's only thirty miles away. It is located on the Yockanookani River."

"Do you think we'll be welcome there?"

Nashoba shrugged. "Red Dog is the *Miko*, the district chief of that area. He is a good friend of my father. I don't think we'll have any trouble."

Hannah didn't say anything, just nodded in agreement to everything Nashoba suggested. Zeb had the feeling that she and Nashoba had already discussed the plan. He couldn't imagine when that would have been possible.

He, too, nodded in agreement. "All right, let's give it a try. I would feel much safer camping with you in a Choctaw village than I would on the Natchez Road."

Nashoba and Hannah exchanged looks and Hannah smiled. "It's all settled, then," he said.

They reached the outskirts of the village late in the afternoon. Nashoba stopped and pointed to the river. "Before we meet the Miko and the Alikchi, let's wash and change our clothes. The horses need a bath, too."

They walked the horses to the riverbank, followed by some of the village children. Zeb untacked Christmas and led him to the river.

Hannah had already led Harlequin into the cool water. He began pawing the water, throwing up great splashes. Then, with a groan of pleasure, the little horse sank to his knees in the shallow water and rolled onto his side.

Christmas pawed at the water, but when he dropped to his knees and rolled over, his huge bulk created a wave that soaked Hannah. She laughed and called to Harlequin. The horses stood up and shook themselves off. Nashoba and Zeb led them back to the grassy bank to graze. The village children stood in a solemn cluster, watching what they were doing.

Nashoba pointed downstream. "Hannah," he said. "There's a nice pool, not too deep, just around the curve of the river. Why don't you go down there, and Zeb and I will wash here?"

"It's within hollering distance," he shouted to Hannah, as an afterthought.

He turned to Zeb to explain. "Bears or big cats aren't likely to come this close to the village," he said, "but you can never be sure."

After washing, Zeb just wanted to relax and enjoy the water. Nashoba had already bathed and changed his clothes. Zeb looked up to see Hannah and Nashoba standing on the bank, watching him. Hannah, with her short hair and butternut-colored pants and shirt, looked like a young boy. "You saw the council house in that little clearing next to the village?" Nashoba asked. Zeb nodded. "Hannah and I will go up and talk with the chief about spending the night here," Nashoba continued. "Stay as long as you like and enjoy yourself."

When Zeb got back to the clearing, a dozen horses stood tethered to the rail. The strong smell of horse sweat told Zeb that some of these horses had been ridden a distance to get here. There was something different about the horses, he noticed. They were stockier, stronger looking, and broader in the hindquarters than most Indian ponies. These must be the famous Choctaw ponies his grampa was always talking about. He wondered how fast they were.

Men were moving into the clearing, coming from every direction. When they glanced at him, he nodded. No one seemed surprised to see him. Most of them nodded back, and a few of them smiled in a way that made Zeb check to be sure his pants hadn't split open again.

Hannah and Nashoba came running out of the council house. Hannah seemed to be bursting with news, but she waited for Nashoba to say something. He looked at Zeb very seriously. "The Miko wants to talk with you. Come now. He is waiting."

"What's going on? Why are there so many people here?"

"This is the day, once a year, that the villages decide who will be the leading brave, the one who will lead the others into battle with the Chickasaw or the Creek if they attack. The important thing now is that the Miko wants to talk with you."

He looked so serious, Zeb was worried. Maybe they shouldn't have asked to stay here. He looked over at Hannah. She was grinning. Zeb relaxed. It couldn't be that bad.

Zeb walked between Nashoba and Hannah back to the council house. They entered through a large, heavy door. The building was similar to the council house at Yowani except that this one had a dirt floor. It had one large room, no furniture at all, and a single small window at the center of each wall.

At least fifteen men stood looking at him. He learned later that the men were the chiefs of the surrounding villages. It was easy to know which person was the Miko. A man about thirty years old, he was tall and slender and stood proudly erect. He looked to be very much in charge.

Nashoba whispered to Zeb, "Walk over and stand in front of the Miko. He will ask you some questions. Answer them all as honestly as you can."

Zeb licked his lips. He shifted his weight from one foot to the other. This seemed to be an inquiry of some kind—maybe about Hannah. He wondered what would happen if they didn't like his answers.

Zeb stood in front of the Miko with his arms hanging loosely at his side. He tried to look more at ease than he felt. The Miko stared at him solemnly. "I understand," he said, "that you saved Hannah from the Mason gang?"

"No, sir," Zeb said. "She had run away and we just traveled together. She deserves all the credit for getting away from them."

"But you did save her from drowning?"

"Well, sir," Zeb said, "we wouldn't have been in that river if we hadn't been running away from some people looking for me. I made the decision to try to swim the horse across. I got her into it, and I had to get her out. None of that was her fault." Zeb thought about those moments when he wasn't really sure that he should go after her.

"You tried to focus the attention of the army patrol on you so Hannah could escape?"

Zeb was feeling very uncomfortable. They made it sound much more heroic than it really was. He hadn't thought that either one of them had had much of a chance.

Zeb was about to say something, but the Miko held up his hand. "And you told Hannah that you would be proud to be a Choctaw?"

Zeb nodded. Had he made a fool of himself?

By this time all of the other chiefs had gathered behind the Miko. They looked very serious indeed.

The Miko stared at Zeb for a long time, and then he said, "We have decided to make you an honorary brave in the Choctaw Nation. If you agree, you will be as a brother to all of us, and we will be your brothers. When you are in the Choctaw lands, you will be subject to the laws of the Choctaw and the direction of the village chief."

The Miko locked his eyes with Zeb's. "Do you want to be a Choctaw?"

Zeb was very honored, but he couldn't find the words to express his feelings. He nodded his head.

"Good!" the Miko said. "The ceremony will begin."

Zeb stepped back to stand between Nashoba and Hannah. "So this is what you were up to at Choteau's Inn," he whispered.

Nashoba put his hand on Zeb's shoulder. "I, for one, am proud to call you brother."

Hannah's eyes were shining. She seemed very happy.

Zeb watched Hannah turn and walk away, slipping through the crowd of men and out the door, little clouds of red dust rising from her footsteps. Nashoba whispered to Zeb, "She had to leave. The ceremony is only for men."

Nashoba gestured with his chin at an old man who was moving to the center of the room. He was being helped by two of the village chiefs.

"He's the Alikchi," Nashoba whispered. "He is more of a priest than a doctor. He calls on the Great Spirit who created us all."

"Today," Nashoba whispered, "you are being born as a Choctaw. You will get a Choctaw name. The Alikchi will give it to you. He will be inspired by the Great Spirit. The Great Spirit will also tell you what to do with your life. Listen carefully. I will tell you what he is saying."

The old man began to speak. His voice was low and clear, in spite of his age. "In the beginning," he said, "the Choctaw came from far away in the West, across the great water. No one knows from where. They traveled with their leader, *Chata*, and a white dog of great magical powers. They carried with them the bones of their ancestors. They found this place and decided to stay, building the sacred mound, *Nanih Waiya,* to be the center of our nation.

"They separated themselves from others, the Natchez, the Chickasaw, and the Muscogee. Those are tribes of violence. The Choctaw is a tribe of peace. This tribe will fight only to defend its land or to protect its honor.

"The Choctaw divorced some but welcomes others, men of great courage and of peace.

"The Great Spirit is poured upon you, Zebulon D'Evereux. Your Choctaw name is *Isuba Nakni,* 'Brave Horse,' in honor of the courage you have shown. It will be up to you, Brave Horse, and to the other young men of the Choctaw nation to make sure that we keep our word and show to all of the other nations that we are people of honor."

Suddenly all of the village chiefs began shouting in Choctaw and pushing their way toward Zeb. The noise was deafening. Dust from the dirt floor filled the air. The men pounded Nashoba on the back and grabbed Zeb and hugged him. Only a few of the men spoke English. They all seemed to have one question: *"Ishtaboli?"*

Nashoba laughed. "No, they don't really expect you to play ishtaboli. At least, not till you've practiced for a while. It's traditional after a ceremony for the men and sometimes the women to play ishtaboli. You would be better off as a spectator."

"But I learn pretty quickly." Zeb protested. "Tell me how to play—"

"Even though this will only be a ritual game, with just a few on each side, probably no more than thirty, it still would be better for you to watch," Nashoba explained. "Sometimes we have over a hundred on each side! We may be men of peace, but we play ishtaboli very, very violently."

Suddenly all the village chiefs began shouting in Choctaw and pushing their way toward Zeb.

Nashoba laughed at the disappointed look on Zeb's face. "You will thank me later. This will be a very short game because there will be horse racing after the ishtaboli."

Zeb relaxed. Horse racing. He wondered if the Choctaw ever bet on the races. Maybe he could double what money he had left.

After being hugged and pounded by everyone there, Zeb and Nashoba left the council house and found Hannah just outside the door. She looked up expectantly.

Zeb was about to speak, but Nashoba held up his hand. "Remember, a Choctaw never tells his name to anyone. Someone else must do it."

He put his hand on Zeb's shoulder and turned to Hannah. "His name," he said proudly, "is Isuba Nakni, Brave Horse."

CHAPTER THIRTEEN

Ishtaboli

Hundreds of Choctaw moved through the forest toward a broad field—about fifteen acres of flat meadow, the grass cropped short by the horses. Two tall poles several yards apart served as goalposts at each end of the field. Men were beginning to gather for the game.

Nashoba stopped and took off his shirt and his pants. All he had on was a cloth between his legs and a belt around his waist to hold it up. Something about the way he stood—knees slightly bent, weight on the balls of his feet, ready to move— reminded Zeb of a wild animal. His head was still, but his eyes were moving, taking in the other players. Nashoba handed Hannah a hank of horse tail which she hooked into the back of his belt.

A young Choctaw brave handed two strange-looking sticks to Nashoba. Hannah said they were called *kapuchas*. They looked like long wooden spoons. They were about three feet long, made of white oak and split on the end. The split piece was bent back and lashed to the main part of the stick, forming a pocket the size of a cupped hand. A leather thong was strung across the back of the pocket.

Nashoba's teammate tossed him a heavy, leather-covered ball the size of an apple, which Nashoba caught in the pocket of one of the sticks. He tossed the ball back and forth between the two sticks and then threw it hard to his teammate. The other player caught it and tossed it on the ground in front of Nashoba. Nashoba ran to the ball, scooped it up in a stick, and threw it back to his teammate.

Someone beat a drum, and another person blew into a cane flute. The two teams, about thirty men each, ran to the center of the field. Hannah told Zeb that the night before, the team members and some of the women had danced the Ball Play Dance. In the dance the players rattle their kapuchas together violently and sing loudly to the Great Spirit. The women dance between them chanting.

"Today," she said, "after this ritual game and the horse racing they will probably dance the Eagle Dance." She cocked her head and looked up at him out of the corners of her eyes. "Maybe they'll invite you to participate."

Four of the Alikchis sat on one side, smoking long pipes, blowing smoke slowly into the air. Hannah said that they were the judges of the play and were sending smoke to the Great Spirit asking for guidance.

An old man walked to the center of the field. He raised his hand. The group was suddenly quiet. After a moment, he threw the ball into the air.

Most of the men crushed together in the middle, trying to find the ball and whacking each other with the sticks. They screamed at each other. Suddenly, someone erupted from the group, running with the ball. It was Nashoba! As he ran toward one of the goalposts, he held the stick up the air, twisting it back and forth to keep the ball juggling in the pocket, ready to be thrown. At least ten men closed in on him. They swung their sticks at him as hard as they could. Zeb was convinced that if they ever connected with him, they would kill him.

Suddenly Nashoba stopped, and in one motion he wheeled and threw the ball to a teammate across the field. Most of the men chased after the teammate. A few, however, seemed to be content to stay with Nashoba, trying to club him with their sticks. Fortunately, most of the blows fell on the shafts of the sticks.

The players were trying to throw the ball between the goalposts of the opponents. Whenever they were successful, the two teams assembled again in the middle to fight over the ball again.

Several players had to be helped off the field. Most of them had bloody noses. Hannah told him that in the big games between two villages bones were sometimes broken.

A cloud of dust rose over the field. Zeb could smell the sweet aroma of dried manure. *They must use this field for the horse racing as well,* he thought. The dust was so thick that it was now impossible to pick out Nashoba from among the players. He wondered how they could see the ball.

On one side, a long line of women sat on the ground with little piles of goods in front of them: baskets, sleeping mats, deerskins, beaded belts, piles of fruits and sweet potatoes. Zeb pointed to them. "Are they going to sell those things after the game?" he asked.

Hannah sighed. "I was hoping you wouldn't notice," she said. "Those women are betting on which team will win. They bet the crafts they have made or the food they have gathered or grown. They take these games very seriously."

Most of the men crushed together in the middle, trying to find the ball and whacking each other with the sticks.

Suddenly a shout of victory came from one of the teams. The players all piled their kapuchas behind the goal they had defended and then gathered in a large circle in the center of the field. Hannah put her hand on Zeb's arm. "Brave Horse," she said, "if you are going to enter the horse races, you better go out to the field. But please don't make any wagers."

"Is that why you didn't want me to notice?"

"This isn't like any horse race you have ever seen."

Zeb doubted that there could be a horse race unlike any he had ever seen before.

He was sure that there was no horse race he couldn't win.

Gentling the Horses

Nashoba handed Zeb a loincloth and a leather belt similar to the ones Nashoba and the others wore to play ishtaboli. "You better get ready," Nashoba shouted over the noise. "Looks like the village of Red Dog has chosen you to race."

Zeb tried not to let his face show what he felt. Obviously Nashoba didn't think much of Christmas as a racehorse. Well, he thought, Nashoba and Hannah were in for a big surprise.

Zeb looked up at the bright sun. Early afternoon. A little hot for racing, but Christmas had raced when it was hotter.

In the midst of the crowd, some of the older boys were already taking off their shirts and pants to put on the loin-cloths. No one seemed to pay any attention to the naked young men. Zeb thought about changing the way they were doing it, but at the last minute, he lost his nerve. He ran over to the edge of the forest, stood behind a bush, took off his pants and shirt, and put on the loincloth and belt as quickly as he could.

He ran back to Hannah, handed her his clothes, and continued toward the open field. "Get Christmas for me," he called to her. "Someone can help you with the saddle." Hannah just stood there and smiled at him, his clothes tucked under her arm. Nashoba shouted as he trotted alongside Zeb toward the center of the field, "The Choctaw don't use saddles."

Zeb wondered how he would do, racing against people who never used saddles. Riding bareback would be no advantage to him now.

The braves formed a huge circle around the field. Each of the six villages was allowed to choose one rider. The men of the village of Red Dog, to which Zeb now belonged, all but pushed him into the center of the circle.

The Alikchi was helped onto the field. He held up his hand, and when it was silent he sucked on his long pipe and blew three puffs of smoke into the air. Then he began to chant. Nashoba whispered, "He is calling on the Great Spirit.… 'Oh Great Spirit,'" he translated, "'give each of these, our braves, the courage and the skill and the strength to win. Protect them from harm. Guide them that they compete in this and in all things with honor.'"

The other riders ran in place and flexed their muscles. The boy nearest Zeb looked at him with a clear challenge in his eyes. The Alikchi began to instruct the racers. Nashoba translated. "He is saying that you will each gentle your horse, and then ride it from here to the poles at the east end and then around the poles on the west end, returning to the center. The first one to cross the stick he will place on the ground will be the winner."

It certainly sounded simple enough. This was just a country road race, a lot like the races in Franklin. He kept looking back at the council house. *When will I be able to go and get Christmas?* he wondered. He shuffled his feet in the fine dust, wishing that they would finish with the ceremony and get on with the race. He told himself that he was not nervous, but his mouth felt dry.

The old man was helped to the sidelines. Everyone was looking toward the council-house clearing. Six young braves ran toward them, each one leading a horse. The horses rolled their eyes and danced away from their handlers.

Zeb whispered to Nashoba. "What's going on?"

Nashoba grinned at Zeb's surprise. "Those are the horses you and the others will ride. They have never been ridden. I wouldn't have bet that you could do it, but Hannah thinks you can."

"Where did they get them?"

"We breed our horses. You saw some of them tied up near the council house. If any of the colts aren't exactly what the breeders want for size, build, and temperament, they save them for these games. No one is allowed to ride them. These horses are more like the Chickasaw horses than ours."

Zeb looked over at Hannah. She was grinning. Did she really think he could gentle an unbroken horse and then ride it in a race? He had helped his grampa gentle a lot of horses. It usually took hours just to get them used to his voice and his hand on their backs. *This contest is going to go on a long time,* he thought, *before anyone will be racing down that field.*

Each horse had a simple leather noose around the nose, with another thong running up behind the ears to hold the nose strap on. A pair of leather leads attached to the back of the noose, to serve as reins. This form of bridle was similar to the hackamore they sometimes used on the farm. The hackamore was far from painless, but it didn't damage the horse's mouth the way some bits did.

Five of the six wild horses were bays. They looked strong and healthy. The sixth was a dark gray, broader in the hindquarters than the others and much stockier. He stood at least sixteen hands high. The horse fought the handler all the way onto the field.

The other horses were now more or less calm, but the big one still danced around and tried to pull away from his handler. He kicked out at the other horses whenever they moved near him, and then ran in circles around the handler. Zeb shook his head in admiration. *If anyone can gentle that animal without getting killed,* he thought, *he'll never let another horse pass him in a race.*

The Miko held out a handful of straws and each of the boys chose one. The young brave who had picked the shortest straw got to choose which horse he wanted, and he went directly to the big horse.

Zeb kicked the dirt, raising a cloud of fine red dust. His teeth were clamped tightly together. He would have loved to work with that spirited horse.

The boy took the leather lead from the handler and began to walk the big horse back toward the other braves. The horse reared, almost lifting the boy off the ground. He trotted in circles around the young brave, kicking out his hind feet. He reared again. The boy leaped to one side as the horse's front hooves narrowly missed him. The boy pulled hard on the leather thongs, leading the horse back to the handler. He then chose one of the bays.

The other two braves who had drawn short straws looked over all of the remaining horses, but they ignored the big gray.

Zeb couldn't fault their reasoning. The big, powerful horse would probably be faster in a race, but he might take a lot longer to gentle enough to ride.

Zeb was the fourth to choose. In spite of his misgivings, he walked directly to the big horse. He took the leather thongs from the handler and tried to lead the horse back to where the six riders had been standing. The horse turned his head, looking down at Zeb, his eyes wide and daring. Zeb stroked his neck, trying to control him by pulling gently on the thongs. The horse jerked his head away, almost tearing the lines from Zeb's hand. Zeb held on and turned back toward the other braves, walking slowly forward as the horse danced behind him.

When the sixth horse had been chosen, the Miko raised his arm and then lowered it. Nashoba shouted to Zeb, "That's the signal to start the race."

Zeb loosened the noose slightly. He began to stroke the horse, talking to it quietly. "Calm down. Atta boy. Calm down. You can do it. Not gonna hurt you. Calm down."

For a moment the horse stood quietly, then he yanked his head up, almost lifting Zeb off the ground. Zeb tried to act as if nothing unusual had happened.

He continued to talk to the horse and stroke its long nose and cheek. When he moved his hand back down the neck, the horse danced away from him. Zeb looked around at the other riders. They were doing the same thing he was, talking quietly to the horses. The two nearest him didn't seem to be talking as much as simply making low guttural sounds. Their horses were a little calmer than his.

Zeb placed his hand on the horse's back and walked around with him as he circled. When the horse stopped prancing, Zeb pressed his hand down on the horse's back, still talking quietly to him. "That's all right. Good boy!"

Zeb kept talking and touching the horse. He stroked the horse from the withers to the middle of his back. Zeb leaned his chest against the side of the horse, mixing his sweat with the horse's. Then he turned once again to the head, running his hands down the face, talking quietly. He ran his hand over the soft muzzle, then back up, slipping his fingers under the thong to loosen it even more.

There was a sudden roar and then laughter. The big horse pulled hard on the leather thongs, dancing away from Zeb. He held on and looked over to where the other boys were working with their horses. One of them had tried to mount and was immediately thrown.

What made that fool try so soon? It usually took hours of work with the horse to be able to mount the first time and even more time and patient training before you could ride it.

The horse that had thrown the young brave wasn't able to run very far. A huge circle of Choctaw men and women stood along the sidelines of the playing field. As the horse approached them, they lifted their hands and shouted. The horse turned and ran along the side of the field.

A mounted Choctaw brave burst onto the field, raced alongside the frightened horse and threw a leather lasso over his head. The boy ran over to retrieve it from him.

All of Zeb's efforts to calm the horse now seemed to have been wasted. His horse was dancing again and kicking his hind legs. Zeb's muscles ached. He wondered how long he would be able to keep this up.

The horse jerked his head away, almost tearing the lines from Zeb's hand.

CHAPTER FIFTEEN

The Race

Zeb decided to start over. "Calm down. Calm down," he whispered. "Everything's gonna be all right. Atta boy. Calm down." He stroked the horse as he led it in a circle and then changed direction.

One by one, the boys vaulted onto the horses and then slipped off again. Zeb did the same. "There," he said, "that wasn't so bad was it?"

He loosened the thong a little more. He knew that the noose would give him control, but he wanted to reduce the possibility of hurting the horse as much as possible.

Zeb continued to talk with the horse. He led him around in a larger and larger circle, first going clockwise and then counterclockwise. He ran ahead of the horse until the horse was moving at a fast trot, and then he suddenly stopped and held the thongs until the horse stopped running in a circle around him. "Good boy!" he whispered. "You did it!"

He stroked the horse again and vaulted on and off several times. The horse seemed less frightened of him, more trusting.

Zeb led him again, running in front and suddenly turning to the left or the right, pulling a rein hard as he did so. The horse began to anticipate him, turning before he pulled the rein.

Zeb relaxed for a moment. His muscles didn't seem to ache as much. He smiled for the first time since the race had begun, whispering to the horse, "You are quite a horse, my friend. I'd like to take you home with me."

He could taste on his lips a salty mixture of sweat and dust, so familiar to him from the long hours he worked beside his grandfather. He ran his hand across his face, trying to keep the sweat from burning his eyes.

He vaulted onto the horse's back and stayed there for a moment while the horse danced sideways, and then he slipped off. He tried it again and again, each time staying on a little longer. Finally, he vaulted on and pulled the right rein lightly. The horse ignored him at first and then it turned right and trotted in a large circle. Zeb slipped off. He patted the horse. "Good boy!" he whispered. "You're almost ready."

He thought that he had better see how the others were doing. He knew he could learn a lot from them. Nashoba had told him that Running Bear, the brave working next to him, was the oldest and most skilled of the group. He had been one of the six boys, along with Nashoba, who had been chosen by Nashoba's father to be taught how to read and write English. If he won today, he was in line to be the head brave of the district. Zeb was determined to make him work for it.

When Running Bear looked up and saw Zeb watching him, he turned his back as if he didn't want Zeb to see what he was doing. He vaulted onto the horse and urged him around in a circle, just as Zeb had done. Then he pulled on the other thong and the horse turned and circled the other way.

Zeb noticed that the shadows from the western posts stretched long across the field now. He looked at the huge crowd gathered along the sides of the field. Most of the spectators had long been seated on the ground. He saw Hannah and Nashoba in the front row, watching him.

He couldn't resist the temptation. He swung up on his horse again and tried to make the horse do a figure eight. In the middle of the maneuver, his horse twisted suddenly, and Zeb found himself on the ground. He still had hold of the reins, though. He was sure that his face was red. *They must think I'm a greenhorn,* he thought.

He got up and talked calmly with the horse as if being thrown off was what he had expected. "Good boy!" he said. "You are one clever horse." He stroked the animal's muzzle and then vaulted on once more.

Immediately the horse twisted again, but this time Zeb was ready for him. He relaxed and moved with the horse, and then he steered him to circle in one direction and then the other. He looked over at Running Bear, whose body was also glistening with sweat.

Running Bear was still working with his horse, vaulting on and off and making circles. Mounting again, Running Bear looked over his shoulder at Zeb and then suddenly turned his horse toward the posts at the end of the field. Running Bear squeezed his legs and released the pressure on the leather noose. His horse moved from a fast trot to a full gallop, running hard toward the goalposts. The onlookers at that end of the field scrambled up and out of the way to give the horse plenty of room. The race was on!

Zeb wasn't sure that his horse was ready, but he couldn't resist the challenge. He squeezed his legs around the horse and chased after Running Bear. Just as Zeb expected, the horse seemed to be as competitive as he was. The horse raced after Running Bear, thundering toward the crowd at the end of the field. Zeb began to pull back a bit on the thongs, worrying about making the sharp turn around the goalposts. These horses had never raced before. They didn't know anything about making a sharp turn with riders on their backs. The horse didn't slow down at all. If anything, he galloped harder.

Running Bear had reached the posts and was trying to make his horse come around. The horse was fighting the leather noose, his head turned to the left but his body still going straight. He was running away with the rider! They were at the edge of the forest.

Running Bear pulled back hard on the leather thongs. The horse began to slow down. By this time, Zeb had reached the goalposts. He pulled on the left rein and leaned to the left at the same time. His horse responded to the pressure of the thong and Zeb's legs, just as he had learned in the hours of gentling, making a sharp left around the goalposts. Zeb hoped that Running Bear could see their turn.

But just as the horse was in the sharpest part of the turn, Zeb felt the horse slip. The hind leg was going out from under him! There was no way to stop it. Zeb leaped off just as the horse fell.

He rolled over and then ran to the horse, grabbing the reins as the horse scrambled back on his feet. Zeb walked the horse back and forth, stroking the animal. The horse's neck was covered in lather and he was breathing hard. His eyes were wide once again, watching Zeb. Zeb spoke calmly to the horse. "That's all right," he said. "That was my fault. Too sharp a curve. We'll have to work on that."

There was no way to stop it. Zeb leaped off just as the horse fell.

Zeb looked up. Running Bear was riding by him, headed toward the other goalposts. He waved his arm at Zeb. "Come on," he shouted.

Two of the other boys had started to ride toward him. They barely had their horses under control. It would take them a while to get to the first turn.

"Are you all right, boy?" Zeb asked the horse.

He ran his hand down each leg to make sure the horse hadn't injured himself. Then he slowly trotted him around in a small circle to see if the horse favored any leg.

When he didn't see any sign of damage, he vaulted back on the horse and raced toward the other goalposts. Running Bear was already halfway down the field. Zeb squeezed his legs tighter and the horse responded. Zeb wondered if they would be able to catch up to Running Bear. He urged his horse even more, but the distance between them remained the same. At the other goalpost, Running Bear leaped off his horse and led him around in a circle. When Zeb caught up with him and rounded the post, Running Bear swung back up. "Now we race," he said.

Why had Running Bear waited for him to catch up? he wondered. Zeb knew that he himself wouldn't have waited for anyone. He squeezed his legs once again. To Christmas that was the signal to take off and fly. But the horse didn't seem to need the signal. He was running at a full gallop.

But Running Bear kept his horse just in front of Zeb's. No matter which side Zeb tried to pass him on, Running Bear's horse was there, in the way. The two horses galloped across the finish line with Running Bear ahead by a length.

It took half a field for the horses to slow down to a walk and return to the center.

Everyone was screaming and laughing. The two riders pulled up in front of the old Alikchi, who was standing near the stick he had placed on the ground. The boys slipped off the horses and stood in front of him. Running Bear said something in Choctaw. The Alikchi put up his hands. "We will wait for the others," he said in English.

The other four boys rode their horses back to the center of the field and dismounted. Two of the horses were still turning from one side to the other. The old man looked at Zeb, as if he were disappointed in him. "It is no honor for a Choctaw brave to win if his opponent just gives up. Did you think that we would be pleased if you let Running Bear win?"

Zeb could hardly speak. "What do you mean?" he croaked.

The old man pointed down the field toward the goalposts, "Why didn't you continue after your horse fell?"

That was a question he could answer. "I have been taught, sir, to take care of the horse, to be sure it is all right, to give it a little time to recover before mounting again. It could have pulled a tendon or broken a bone. Better to lose a few minutes. The horse is always more important than the race."

The Alikchi looked at Zeb a long time, as if weighing what he was saying. Finally he nodded. "Everything the Choctaw brave does with horses," he said, "he does with the knowledge that we have many horses. We breed them."

He gestured toward the six horses. "These horses are of little importance to us except as food. We save them for these races and then we let the children play with them. In a contest, a brave must never give up. If his horse falls, he gets back on. If it is hurt, he tries to ride it anyway. If the animal cannot go on, the brave must finish the race on another horse. The horse is not important. Winning the contest is."

The old man ran his eyes over the six contestants. "Running Bear and all the rest of us want to be sure that you were not giving away the race for some reason."

"I would never do that, sir. I love to win."

The Alikchi smiled. He seemed to be relieved. "Brave Horse," he said, "you gentle the horse like a Choctaw. In many ways, you ride like a Choctaw brave. I am happy that you are an honorary member of the Choctaw Nation."

The old man turned to Running Bear, speaking in Choctaw. Nashoba stood next to Zeb, translating what the old man was saying. "Running Bear, you have won the race! The Council of Chiefs will decide tonight if you will become the leading brave of the district." He put a long leather thong around Running Bear's neck. Tied to the thong were dozens of long hairs from a horse's tail.

CHAPTER SIXTEEN

Kapucha

Hannah and Nashoba were standing behind the Alikchi. Hannah held Zeb's clothes in a tight, neat bundle under her arm. She was smiling. Zeb had the feeling that the race was as important to her as it was to him. He suddenly remembered that he was standing there practically naked, wearing only the loincloth and the big belt.

He was still holding on to the leather thongs of the horse. He held them out. "Sir?" he asked. "What shall I do with the horse?"

The Alikchi shrugged his shoulders. "Whatever you like," he said. "It is your horse. The riders who finish the race get to keep their horses."

"But, sir!" Zeb said. "I can't take your horse."

The Alikchi frowned. "Why not?" he asked. "We have plenty of horses. If you want the horse, it is yours."

Zeb reached up and stroked the sweat-streaked horse. "Well," he said to the horse, "what do you think of that? You're *my* horse. I told you I wanted a horse like you. Think I'll call you Kapucha."

The Alikchi stared at Zeb. "Are you sure you are not part Choctaw?" he said.

Zeb grinned. "I am now, sir."

They were interrupted by the pounding of another drum, a hollow log with a piece of deerskin stretched across the opening. Hannah grabbed his hand, pulling him toward the sound. "C'mon," she said, "you still have time to join the Eagle Dance."

Zeb remembered the look on her face earlier when she had suggested that he might want to participate. He shook his head. "No," he said. "I think I'll just watch."

They sat on the grass, he and Nashoba still in their loincloths. It was cooler now that the sun was going down. Hannah sat between them. For the first time since he had met Hannah, she seemed to be really happy.

Four groups of four men each approached the center of the field. They wore only loincloths and headdresses made of eagle feathers. Their bodies were covered with white clay. Each man carried an eagle feather.

The leading man of each group pushed a spear into the ground. Then, at the beat of the drum, each of the leading men began to dance, squatting down as low as possible and then leaping into the air. They hopped and then squatted and jumped again. When one of them became exhausted, he went to the end of his group's line, and the next man performed the same series of squats, jumps, and hops.

"I'm glad they didn't invite me to join in," Zeb shouted over the noise.

Nashoba stood up and started walking toward the council house. He laughed. "Don't worry," he called over his shoulder. "Only certain braves are selected to perform the Eagle Dance. It takes a lot of practice and incredible stamina."

Zeb turned and looked down at Hannah. She was smiling.

It was almost dark. Zeb could smell meat cooking. He looked toward the council house. Spirals of smoke rose from several cooking fires. He stood up. "C'mon," he said to Hannah, "I'm starving!"

Hannah got to her feet in one graceful motion. "In the Choctaw Village," she said, "the women serve the men, especially during the annual games. It would not be right for you to go to the cook fires and serve yourself. Just sit here for a few more minutes. I'll bring you some food."

She put his bundle of clothes on the ground and moved toward the cook fires.

He decided to change into his shirt and pants just the way everyone else did. He took off the loincloth and slipped on his pants. No one seemed to pay any attention to him. The dust in the air had mixed with the sweat on his body, creating rivulets of brown mud running down his chest and legs.

He was pulling his shirt over his head when he noticed a young girl in a beautiful Choctaw dress walking slowly toward him. She had the erect posture and smooth movement of the women Zeb had seen who were used to carrying heavy loads on their heads.

She wore a long deerskin dress which hardly moved as she strode. The upper part of the dress had a high neck, and around her waist she wore a wide belt made of thousands of tiny beads. A shawl covered her head. She carried a drinking gourd in one hand and a large piece of venison on a stick in the other. As she got closer, Zeb just stared at her. It was Hannah!

He couldn't take his eyes off her. What a change from her ragged clothes! She offered him the gourd. He thanked her for the drink and put it to his lips. Sweet and rich, it tasted like ground-up corn and honey.

Now that the men had all been fed, the women were beginning to serve themselves. Hannah sighed. "At last," she said. "I'm starved." She handed him the meat and hurried back to the cook fires.

Zeb leaned back on his elbows. *This is a lot like a church picnic in Franklin,* he thought. *The women prepare all of the food. They serve everyone else, and then they have a chance to eat.*

After the meal, the older men sat together talking in low voices. As the stars began to show, a stillness settled over the scattered groups. The boisterous noise that was part of the games and the horse racing was replaced now by a quiet, low murmur, broken only by occasional squeals from the very young children still chasing each other.

He would have to be on his way tomorrow. He knew that Hannah wanted to go with him, but she was so safe and happy here. It would be even more risky for her to travel with him now. Not only were McPhee's men somewhere on the road, but the sergeant was after him, too.

He looked up as Nashoba sat down next to him. "I hope," Nashoba said, "that you and Hannah can stay a few days."

"Won't be any time for that. I really have to leave tomorrow. I want to talk with you about maybe leaving Hannah here, she—"

Nashoba held up his hand. "Wait," he said. "I have a lot to tell you."

"But the trip will be dangerous. She can go back with—"

"I've already talked with her. I don't think that anything will convince her to stay. She hasn't seen her parents in more than six months. They think she's dead."

"I figured she'd feel that way," Zeb said. "But it will be a little slower with Kapucha, and it will be harder now to hide than it has been—"

Nashoba interrupted again. "I have decided to go with you," he said. "I know that trail very well. We'll travel to Washington the way the Choctaw do. We use the Natchez Road only when we have to. No one ever sees us."

"But I will want to stop at each stand to see if they have seen my grampa. He might be going north as I am going south."

"We can easily do that."

"There will be three of us then, with four horses."

"The Miko has agreed to let us have all of the grain we can carry and all of the food we want as well. If you can get Kapucha to work as a packhorse, we can carry enough to feed ourselves and the horses for the whole trip."

"Kapucha isn't even broken in. There's a lot of work still to be done."

"I know. I know. You could ride him a bit more this evening, and then if we stayed a couple more days and the two of us worked with him, maybe...."

Zeb thought about it. *Will it be possible to have Kapucha ready in just a couple of days? That will delay my search for Grampa. But with the grain, the horses will have more energy than if they depend solely on grass. We might be able to go a few more miles each day. And riding with Nashoba on the Choctaw trails, we'll have a much better chance to get to Natchez safely.*

"All right," Zeb said, "let's give it a try. We'll get Hannah to work with us. She's great with horses."

CHAPTER SEVENTEEN

Homecoming

A week later, when it was almost too dark to ride, they saw the welcoming lights in the windows of the last stand on the Natchez Road, Mount Locust Inn. Zeb knew that this was a place where his grampa never failed to stay when traveling to or from Natchez.

After they set up camp in the deep woods, Zeb rode in alone to speak to the innkeeper. With its smooth, squared-off logs, glass windows, and long porch across the front, the inn looked like the home of a well-to-do farmer. A horse and buggy stood nearby.

Zeb slipped off Christmas and approached the porch stairs just as two men came out of the building. They were wearing city clothes—knee britches with high boots and a waistcoat over a white shirt. One man had on a hat with a tall crown.

Both men turned and stared down at Zeb. "Sorry, son," the innkeeper said. "Got no room, but I can feed ya in about an hour."

The man with the tall hat turned to the innkeeper. "I must be on my way," he said. "I have an important meeting in Natchez."

The innkeeper looked down at Zeb again. "I told you it'd be an hour till the meal is served. You can wait out back."

"I'm sorry to interrupt, sir, but I'm looking for my grampa," Zeb said quickly, before the innkeeper could speak again. "His name is Daniel Ryan. He always stays here. I thought you might have seen him."

The man in the tall hat seemed startled.

"Your grampa's Cracker Ryan?" asked the innkeeper. "Well, I reckon you do look a bit like him, with all that hair. But I ain't seen him in maybe three months."

Zeb sighed and mumbled his thanks. Discouraged, he mounted Christmas. As the innkeeper went back into the inn, the man with the tall hat climbed up into his buggy and motioned to Zeb. Curious, Zeb walked his horse over to the buggy. The man turned in the seat and said to Zeb in a low voice, "Tell me the name of your uncle in Franklin."

"Why, his...his name is Ira Hamilton, sir," Zeb stammered. "But why—how do you—"

The man put up his hand. "I don't have time to explain right now. But here is what you must do. Go down to the docks at Natchez Under-the-Hill when the cotton buyer is in town. Look for a bald man driving a big cotton wagon pulled by four draft horses. He knows where Dan Ryan is. You mustn't tell anyone, and I mean *anyone,* what I have told you, or you may put his life in danger."

"But Grampa's alive? You've seen him?"

The mysterious man looked Zeb straight in the eye. "Be very careful down at Natchez Under-the-Hill," he said. "It's the most dangerous place on the Mississippi." He snapped the reins and steered the horse onto the road toward Natchez.

Zeb watched as the buggy disappeared behind a clump of trees. He clenched his eyes shut. *Grampa's alive! I knew it!* So happy he could hardly contain himself, he urged Christmas back up the trail and turned into the woods, weaving his way through the trees. *Grampa's alive! Grampa's alive!*

I wish I could tell Hannah and Nashoba, he thought. *But I don't even know who that man was or what he was up to. Maybe I'd better wait.*

"Any word of your grampa?" Hannah asked as soon as Zeb rode into camp.

"No," he said, turning his head away. "The innkeeper said he hadn't seen him for months."

Zeb didn't sleep much that night. Before dawn he already had Kapucha loaded with the packs and Christmas saddled and ready to go. He wanted to take Hannah home as he had promised and then head straight for Natchez Under-the-Hill. He had to find his grampa before McPhee's men did.

When Hannah awakened and saw Zeb, she jumped up and shook out her blanket. "I'm sorry, Zeb," she said. "I should have been up early like you. I know how much you want to get to Natchez."

After a quick breakfast, the three travelers set out before the sun came up. When the Natchez Road broke out of the forest, Nashoba was in the lead, his horse in an easy canter. Hannah was just behind him. They were riding on an open road just north of Washington. On their right, they could see the red brick buildings of Jefferson College glowing brightly in the morning sun. Live oak and magnolias stood in rows in a wide meadow.

Nashoba slowed gradually to a walk and then halted in front of the gate. Hannah slowed until Zeb could catch up. Kapucha followed on-lead carrying the heavy packs.

Nashoba swung his arm in a gesture that took in the whole campus. "This is the college I was telling you about, Zeb. I'll stop here and find out what I can."

Hannah started to turn Harlequin back down the road. "I'm less than an hour from home, Nashoba. I can't stop now, even for a minute. You two stay if you want."

Zeb tightened the lead on Kapucha and steered Christmas down the road after Hannah. "Thanks for all your help, Nashoba," he called over his shoulder. "I'm going on with Hannah. Soon as I have a place to leave Kapucha, I'll go looking for my grampa."

Nashoba nodded and waved his hand. "Go on ahead," he said. "I'll try to get to Hannah's house before you leave." He waved again and cantered the horse through the open gate.

This stretch of the road had no shade at all. Zeb began to appreciate the dark forest. Hannah kept pointing to familiar things and yelling over her shoulder. Zeb couldn't hear what she was saying, but he could hear the joy in her voice.

They turned down a long dirt road. Live oaks lined both sides, providing a welcome canopy of cool shade over their heads. Spanish moss draped from the trees.

On both sides of the road, cotton fields stretched as far as they could see, the plants white and heavy with cotton, ready to be picked. Black people pulled long bags between the rows, picking the balls of cotton and stuffing them into the bags. It looked just like the fields in Tennessee except that there were many more slaves here. The farms in the Natchez area were huge. Hannah said the people here called them plantations.

Zeb could see the town of Washington ahead. They passed several houses on both sides of the street, homes a lot like those in Franklin.

On both sides of the road, cotton fields stretched as far as they could see.

Hannah pulled up in front of a small, white house and jumped off Harlequin. She opened the gate and led the horse into the side yard, waving impatiently for Zeb to follow. Zeb slipped off Christmas, took Harlequin's reins, and led the three horses into the yard.

Hannah closed the gate behind them. She looked up at the side of the house and stood on her tiptoes trying to look into the open windows. White curtains moved in the gentle breeze, but it was dark and quiet inside.

Hannah ran around the house to the back porch. Zeb followed, leading the horses. Suddenly Hannah stopped, looking back at Zeb. She seemed unsure of herself, almost frightened.

She walked quietly up the steps and looked in the open windows, first on one side and then on the other. She bent down and peered through the curtains, shading her eyes with her hands. Something she saw inside seemed to overcome her fears. She ran back along the porch and pounded on the door.

Zeb could hear someone calling from inside. "All right! All right! I'm coming. I've told you not to pound the door like that! The doctor don't like it."

Hannah ran back and stood with Zeb in the yard, her fingers digging into his arm. A large black woman dressed in a faded cotton dress with a white apron jerked open the door. She looked surprised to see Hannah and Zeb in the backyard with the horses. She stepped out onto the porch and stood with her hands on her hips, looking down at them. "What do you boys want?" she shouted. "What are you doing back here?"

Then the woman paused, a puzzled look on her face. She walked slowly down the steps and out onto the neatly swept yard until she was a few feet away from Hannah.

Zeb could feel Hannah trembling. She looked up at the woman's face. Suddenly the woman screamed. "It's Miz Hannah! Miz Hannah's come home!"

She reached out her arms, and Hannah lunged into her hug. Zeb heard a woman from inside the house, calling in a loud whisper, "Sarah! What is going on out there? What is all that racket? You know that Dr. McAllister isn't well."

When she came to the door, Zeb knew that she had to be Hannah's mother: a beautiful woman with light tan skin and large black eyes. The woman was wearing an ordinary cotton dress, but her hair was braided in the Choctaw way.

The black woman cried out again, "Miz Martha, it's Miz Hannah!"

Hannah ran to her mother and threw her arms around her waist. Her mother grabbed Hannah's shoulders and held her at arm's length. She stared at Hannah's clothes and shorn hair and then at her upturned face. She collapsed to her knees, throwing her arms around her daughter. Pulling back, she sobbed, "We thought we would never see you again." She hugged Hannah again, squeezing as if she were afraid to let go.

They were both crying. Hannah patted her mother's back. "It's all right, Mama, I'm home."

"Oh, Hannah, I was so scared you were dead. I missed you terribly," her mother said, wiping her hand across her eyes.

Hannah's mother didn't seem to notice Zeb. She took a big breath and got to her feet. She wiped a tear away from her cheek. "Let's go see your father," she said. "He has been feeling poorly ever since we got back to Washington. I know that this is just the medicine he needs."

She pulled Hannah against her hip, patting her back and running her fingers through Hannah's shaggy hair. Then she took Hannah's hand, turned, and walked quickly and quietly into the house. Hannah looked back at Zeb and waved at him to follow them.

Hannah's mother opened a door to what looked to be a laboratory. A tall, lean man was sitting at a table, looking through a microscope. Zeb could hear Hannah's mother talking quietly to her husband, "Sam. Sam. Hannah is here. She's all right. It really is Hannah."

The man turned his head. He looked almost annoyed. "What did you say?"

"It's Hannah!" her mother cried out. "She's here! She's all right!"

The man slowly stood up and squinted at their silhouettes in the bright sunlight from the open door. He seemed to be much older than Hannah's mother.

Hannah ran to him. "Father! I'm home," she said, hugging his waist.

He looked down at her, frowning as if struggling to guard himself against more pain and hurt. He, too, ran his fingers through her short hair. After a moment, he held her shoulders and looked at her upturned face.

She grinned up at him. "Father! It's me!"

His eyes searched her face. Then he hugged her tightly. "Hannah, my Hannah! It is you." He closed his eyes. "Thank you, Lord," he cried.

Zeb backed out of the house and stood with Sarah on the porch. She rubbed her eyes and said, "I better go in and stir up a little somethin' special for dinner." She looked in at Hannah and her parents.

Christmas stomped a front hoof, switching his tail from one side to the other against the flies. "I guess I'll go unsaddle the horses and take those packs off," Zeb said. "They've been working hard."

Sarah nodded, standing in the doorway and dabbing her eyes with her apron. Zeb led the horses to the barn in back.

There were two other horses in the stables, but neither looked like what he had come to expect of Suba. He welcomed the familiar smells of the clean horse barn: old cedar wood, hay and straw, horse feed, the sweat of horses, fresh manure, leather saddles and bridles, saddle soap.

He untacked Christmas and Harlequin and took the packs off Kapucha. He watered and fed them and then brushed their matted coats. Automatically, as if he were home in Franklin doing his daily chores, he shoveled the fresh manure into a wooden wheelbarrow.

With the chores done, he sat down and leaned against the stable wall. Zeb was tired, and he knew the big horse must be exhausted too. *It would be better to stay overnight,* he thought, *but I can't wait that long.* Christmas lowered his head until his soft nostrils touched Zeb's cheek. Zeb reached up and put his hand gently over the horse's muzzle. "Well, Christmas," he said, "we've brought Hannah home. Soon's we get a little rest, we'll head out for Natchez. We can be there by nightfall."

He could feel the horse's warm breath on his face and neck. "Grampa's hiding out someplace," he said in a low voice. "He doesn't want Tate McPhee and his men to know he's alive. I just hope we can find him before it's too late. Get some rest now, Christmas. We may have a dangerous time ahead of us in Natchez Under-the-Hill."

Zeb leaned his head back and closed his eyes.

To be continued in...

Natchez Under-the-Hill

The fast-paced adventures of Zeb and Hannah continue in this sequel to THE DEVIL'S HIGHWAY.

Zeb encounters unexpected dangers as he tries to uncover clues to his grandfather's whereabouts. Pursued by his enemies and surrounded by the gamblers and thieves who inhabit Natchez Under-the-Hill, Zeb doesn't know whom to trust.

Author's Note

What is the Natchez Trace, and where is it?

This story takes place in 1811 along the Natchez Trace, a five hundred mile long buffalo and Indian trail threading through the wilderness from Nashville to Natchez. The Natchez Trace became a post road when the Chickasaw and Choctaw Indians signed a treaty with President Jefferson in 1801. The U.S. Army was assigned the task of clearing the trail. It worked on the trail for two years but was able to complete only half the job because the trail had so many low, swampy areas and was so heavily overgrown. At the time of this story, the Natchez Road was the most heavily traveled, and the most dangerous, highway in America.

At that time, the highway was called the Natchez Road by those heading south, and that is how it is referred to in this book. People moving north on the highway often called it the Nashville Road or the Boatmen's Trail, and some called it the Chickasaw Trace. The name was changed officially in the 1830s to the Natchez Trace, and that is what it is called today.

Who traveled the Natchez Trace?

Merchants and flat-boaters were the most frequent users of the trail during the time of this story. They would take the trail north on the return leg of their journey.

The best way south was down the rivers to Natchez. Merchants (and farmers) who lived along the remote western frontier wanted to sell their goods and produce in the cities along the southern Mississippi River. Because the Natchez Road wasn't wide or smooth enough for wagons, and because shipping heavy loads by flatboat was much less costly than by wagon, the merchants chose to

This section of the trail, near milepost 45.7, shows how narrow the roadway was and how steep its banks.

use the rivers to transport their goods to Natchez. They would hire crews and build flatboats on the Cumberland, Ohio, or Mississippi Rivers and float their heavy loads up to one thousand miles down the rivers to Natchez, where they sold their goods. They would then break apart the boats and sell the wood as lumber for the homes and buildings in Natchez. Then the merchants and the flatboaters would make their way, on foot or on horseback, back up to Nashville on the Natchez Trace to start the process all over again.

Near the time of this story, many prominent Americans also used the Natchez Trace. Meriwether Lewis, just a few years after returning from his expedition to the Pacific Ocean with William Clark, died of a gunshot wound at the Grinder Stand in October 1809. Andrew Jackson traveled the route frequently, first as a merchant and later, during the War of 1812, as commander of army troops. And, in the 1820s, John James Audubon taught at the women's college in Washington, Mississippi, and traveled the highway frequently.

Merchants and flatboaters used the Natchez Trace heavily until steam-powered paddlewheel boats enabled them to travel up as well as down the strong currents of the Mississippi River and its tributaries.

Who worked the flatboats?

At first, poor farmers and frontiersmen worked as flatboaters. These men were known as Kaintucks, although they were not necessarily from Kentucky. The term was used to refer to mostly uneducated, illiterate backwoodsmen. Later, many of these men became professional boaters who dedicated themselves to moving goods down the Mississippi River. They were rough and ready for hard work, hard drinking, gambling, or a fight. Their pay was about forty or fifty dollars a trip, which they often spent before they left Natchez.

What were the difficulties and dangers on the trail?

Swamps and mud holes made the trail impassable at times. Insects carried debilitating and often fatal diseases. Travelers were attacked by snakes, bears, and cougars, and in the southern portions of the trail, by alligators. Bands of outlaws roamed

A cypress swamp near milepost 122 on the Trace.

the trail, knowing that the returning merchants often carried thousands of dollars in gold and silver, and that the returning boaters had whatever was left of their fifty-dollar pay. The outlaws hid in the forest and robbed and murdered the travelers.

The merchants and flatboaters traveled up the trail in large groups for protection. It was well known that anyone who traveled alone on the trail was seldom seen or heard from again.

Where were travelers able to stay along the trail?

As the number of people traveling the Natchez Trace increased, inns were built along the way. Most of these were simple stands, often not much more than a lean-to with worn and tattered bearskins covering the dirt floor. Letters from early travelers described most of the stands as terrible, stinking, dirty places, and the little food available was often spoiled, rotten, and crawling with insects.

Some of the inns were the farmhouses of settlers. A few of them were quite nice, such as the Jocelyn farm; others were simple log cabins. One of the stands, the Mount Locust

A log cabin typical of the kind travelers might have found along the Natchez Road.

Inn, was very comfortable. It still stands today, the last stop on the Trace before Natchez.

Colbert's Stand, a two-story wooden house, was eventually destroyed by fire, leaving only the stone chimney.

Colbert's Stand, operated by George Colbert on the north side of the Tennessee River, and the Buzzards Inn, operated by Levi Colbert on the south side of the river, were very expensive. The Colbert brothers were well known for their exorbitant prices. George Colbert was reported to have charged the U.S. Army $75,000 to ferry men across the Tennessee River. (The ferries he used were flatboats that had been given to him by the army!)

Were there really that many passenger pigeons in one place?

Yes. The passenger pigeons described at Pigeon Roost migrated to that spot every year. Travelers of the time reported that flocks of these birds would darken the sky. Hundreds

Colbert's Ferry at the Tennessee River was the only way across that wide, sometimes very swift, stretch of water.

of thousands of birds would gather on the branches of the tall trees, and one gunshot could kill dozens of birds. The birds were shot for food and for sport. Shooting the pigeons at Pigeon Roost continued until the late 1800s, when the passenger pigeon population had dwindled to just a few hundred. The passenger pigeon is now extinct, the last one having died in 1914.

What Indians lived near the trail?

The Natchez Trace cut through Chickasaw territory in the north and Choctaw territory in the south. Even though

145

the Natchez Trace went through their territories, the Indians seldom threatened the thousands of whites traveling along the route.

The two tribes were related but had split several generations before this story took place. The Choctaw wished to remain peaceful and agricultural, but the Chickasaw were roaming hunters. The Chickasaw became known for their independence and aggression, especially against the Creek Indians.

Today, young people of the Choctaw living on their ancestral lands near the Trace still play the traditional games passed along by their elders.

In 1830 the U.S. government forced most of the Choctaw to move with the Chickasaw, Creek, and Cherokee across the Mississippi River. Their Trail of Tears took them to the new Indian territories in what is now Arkansas and Oklahoma. The word *oklahoma* means "red man" in Choctaw.

A small band of Choctaw, however, still remains in Philadelphia, Mississippi, not far from the Natchez Trace. The Choctaw there have struggled to maintain their cultural heritage. The young people learn the Choctaw language as well as English in school. They learn the ancient Choctaw dances and music, using the flutes and drums of their ancestors. And they still play ishtaboli, the Choctaw version of lacrosse. They have created an excellent museum on Choctaw history and folklore that is open to the public.

Does the Natchez Trace still exist?

Yes. The narrow dirt highway and the deep unspoiled forest on each side of it have been preserved as a national park. We can drive through the forest from Nashville to Natchez on a quiet paved road parallel to the Natchez Trace. Camp-

The Natchez Trace Parkway, quiet and scenic today, roughly follows the original post road.

grounds are numerous along the route. The U.S. National Park Service maintains a Welcome Center on the Trace at Tupelo, Mississippi, that offers maps and other materials about the Natchez Trace.

To request a free color map of the Natchez Trace Parkway and the old Natchez Trace, call the park service at 800-305-7417, or see the parkway's website at www.nps.gov/natr. The mileage in the map on the inside front cover and on the mileposts shown at the beginning of each chapter of THE DEVIL'S HIGHWAY correspond to those in the parkway map and on the parkway itself. All of the sites in the book can be found on the map.

This National Park Service symbol identifies the Natchez Trace Parkway.

Interested in helping to preserve our national parks?

Write to
The National Parks and Conservation Association
1776 Massachusetts Avenue, NW
Washington, DC 20036